USA TODAY BESTSELLING AUTHOR

ERIN MALLON

The Natural History Novellas

Flirtin'

Chapter One

CALLIOPE

I've always wanted to join the Mile High Club. Picture this: you're soaring through the clouds at thirty-five thousand feet on your way to a luxe vacation. The handsome stranger across the aisle has been making eyes at you the entire flight. So when the lights finally dim and everyone settles back into their neck pillows and *SkyMall* magazines, you down a glass of the airline's finest bubbly, take the hot guy by the hand, and rock it on till the break of dawn.

Actually, my friend Sasha says it's more like trying to squeeze a sausage into its casing while smooshed in a panini press.

But still, it sounds fun and focusing.

And I could really use some focus right now.

I'm a bundle of nerves on a red-eye flight to my first big book signing in Las Vegas.

I pull the headphones down on the sexy, snoring man next to me. "Ralph-alpha," I whisper into his ear.

"Are we there yet?" he rumbles softly, his eyes still closed.

"It's only been an hour since takeoff, sir. You knocked back two whiskeys watching *Rain Man* then passed right out."

His eyes crack open. "They don't call me Ralph-*alpha* for nothing, lady. I am big, brawny man who can hold his liquor."

"Yeah." I laugh at his caveman impression. "For ten minutes tops before you're a sleepy little baby." I rest my head on his shoulder. "Besides, I'm the only one who gets to call you Ralph-alpha."

"And you always will be." He kisses the top of my head, then peers at my open laptop. "You type 'The End' yet?"

"No. Not yet." I scrub my hands over my face. "I think chapter eight, where the Dilophosaurus diddles the Diplodocus, still needs some work."

"The Dilophosaurus *diddles* her?" He chuckles.

I shrug. "You know I like alliteration."

He places a warm hand on my thigh. "Callie. You said you wanted to finish this one before we left so you could enjoy the weekend."

"I know." I scroll backward in my document. "I just think I should just give this chapter one more read-through before—"

He nudges me and gives me the look. The one that says he knows me better than I know myself. Ugh. I love this smug punk so damn much.

"You're right." I sigh. "I'm sure it's fine."

I scroll again, this time to the last page and type the two blessed words every author yearns to type. "The. End."

I place the laptop in the pocket in front of me and crane my neck toward the bathroom entrance, gauging when to make my move.

Damn. The occupied light is on.

When I flop back into the cushy seat, I find Ralph staring at me.

"Proud of you," Ralph says.

"For what? Finishing a book? It's my fifth this year, dude. And it's only April."

"I know. And that's very impressive. Also, who bought their man this first-class flight and trip to Sin City?"

"That would be me," I say proudly. "Can we stop calling it Sin City, though?"

He ignores my request and threads his fingers through mine. "But I meant I'm proud of you for all the changes you've made these past two years. You're... different."

"Different how? Good different? Bad different? Sexy different? What kind of different are we talking about?" I ask the questions, but my attention is still hyper-focused on the closed door several rows back.

An older gentleman exits and shuffles down the aisle.

This is it.

Time to make my move.

"Well, we both know you've always been *sexy* different." Ralph nuzzles my neck, totally unaware of my plans yet still doing plenty to get me into the right headspace. "But, yeah, good different. Chill different."

A teenager rises and makes a beeline for the bathroom, thwarting my plans yet again.

"YOU THINK I'M CHILL RIGHT NOW?!" I say way too loudly.

The woman sitting across the aisle leans forward and huffs dramatically. Ralph shoots her his megawatt smile. She instantly smiles back. I can't blame her for succumbing to his charms. The guy is irresistible.

"Okay, chill was a stretch." Ralph chuckles quietly and wraps his arm around me. "It's probably safe to say you will never be *chill*, but... I guess what I mean to say is..." He struggles to find the right words. "When we first met, it seemed like you had a lot to prove. It's nice seeing you relax into who you really are."

"What can I say? You soothe the savage beast in me."

"Not too much, I hope." He winks. "So. What's going on? You nervous about the signing?"

I scoff. "Of course not. I don't get nervous."

"Callie, everyone gets nervous."

"I've done plenty of book signings before."

"Sure, but they've all been in local bookstores. This thing is huge. Didn't you say there would be over two-thousand people at this one? And Joella Flanders will be there. Even I know that's a big fucking deal. She's the whole reason you started writing in the first place. That has to be at least a little nerve-wracking. If it were me, I'd be a mess. I'd be—"

"Is this your version of a pep talk?" I laugh.

"Sorry, babe." He pauses and looks out the window where a tiny light blinks on the wing tip. "Maybe I'm the nervous one. I don't want to mess anything up for you."

"Ralph. You're the most steady, helpful person I know. I'm psyched you're assisting me. I feel lucky you could pencil me in with your raucous weekend schedule throwing space parties for children."

"You make my new career path sound so sexy," he says.

I snuggle closer. "It *is* sexy. I love how great you are with kids." I pull away slightly and lock concerned eyes with him. "Though that doesn't change my mind about procreating and having actual kids with you myself."

"Oh, I know. We're on the same page about that, milady."

"Excellent." We high-five like dorks.

I'm turning twenty-six next year, and weddings and babies are suddenly popping up all around me. Neither are life paths Ralph and I particularly want to travel down.

It's such a relief knowing we're united on that front.

I make a move to stand at the same moment a mother and her toddler clamber out of their seats. They head straight for the restroom.

"Damn!" I plunk back in my seat and throw up my hands. "Can no one hold their bladders anymore? And why is no one sleeping?"

The lady across the aisle leans forward again. "Perhaps no one is sleeping because *someone* is being so loud."

I smile at her and apologize. It doesn't have the same effect as Ralph's pearly whites.

My mile-high mission temporarily abandoned, I resume sipping champagne and speak quietly to Ralph. "You do realize I'm at least fifty percent responsible for your career change, don't you?"

"Fifty percent?" His eyebrows scrunch together. "More like a hundred. Woman, if you hadn't seduced me on museum property two years ago, I might still be studying the stars and getting planetarium pay."

"Are you complaining?" I bat my lashes at him.

"Never," he says. "Best two years of my life."

"Mine too, baby."

I lean over and plant a kiss on his lips.

"Also," I continue, "let's not forget that what you lost in planetarium pay, you now get in steady sex and a side gig as my audiobook narrator."

"True. And both of those positions are very pleasing to me." The expression on his face changes. "How, um. How are reviews for our first collaborations coming? I'm too scared to look."

I hesitate for a split second. "They're… fine."

I've written over twenty books, and I'm proud of every single one of them.

Some people might call what I do dino porn. But those people would be wrong. My books are beautiful, sensual love stories. The couples just so happen to be extinct prehistoric creatures.

Dinosaurs have been my life and my passion for as long as I can remember. The dream was always to work as a paleontologist at the highest level: guiding patrons in museums, writing scholarly papers, and leading teams of scientists on record-breaking digs.

But life surprises you sometimes.

Two years ago, my secret side gig as *USA Today* Bestselling Author Tracy Triassic became my only gig. Rather than panicking, I decided to embrace it.

And the strangest thing happened.

I discovered that I was the happiest I'd ever been.

The fact that the hot guy next to me wandered his way into my life at approximately the same time certainly contributed to my newfound contentment, but it was more than that. I was finally learning to let go of what I thought I *should* do in life and choose what feels right and good instead.

No matter what anyone else thinks.

But two years in, the newness is starting to wane, and I feel myself falling back into that old habit of looking for outside approval. Of caring what people think.

One thing is certain: readers will tell you what they think.

"Just fine?" Ralph sounds worried.

"The reviews are good!" I chirp. "Great!"

"Oh, thank God." He rests his head against the seat cushion.

Up until now, I hadn't released any of my stories in audio. But when your boyfriend has the hottest voice you've ever heard—seriously, the first time I heard him narrating sexy space facts in the museum planetarium, I almost lost my damn mind—you recognize an opportunity, and you put those dulcet tones to work.

He's been steadily working his way through my backlist, and two weeks ago, I released a whole bunch of audiobooks with him as my narrator.

I rest my head on his shoulder. "You have nothing to worry about, my love. Your rumbly grumbly tones were one of the first things that made me fall for you. My readers will fall for you too."

I'm not being entirely truthful, though. Sure, I hope the reviews are good, and the readers are falling for him, but honestly, I have no clue.

I haven't read any of my reviews in months.

Because I'm a weenie.

A scared little author weenie who's lost her edge.

I miss the days when I wrote on the sly. Back then, I wrote those books for me. I didn't care about reviews or hitting bestsellers lists or being the next "big thing." But ever since I started writing full-time, I feel all this pressure.

I care.

So much.

About everything.

I can read twenty glowing five-star reviews in a row, but it's the nasty one-star review calling me a hack that gets my attention and sticks with me every time.

So I stopped engaging. Took a break from social media and avoided reviews as much as humanly possible. It's helped my emotional well-being big time, but now I feel completely out of touch with my readers.

Did they love my last book?

Did they hate it?

Fuck if I know!

And I have zero ideas of what to expect from this weekend. I could have a line stretching around the block. Or I could be sitting there alone, twiddling my thumbs.

While my boyfriend watches.

I lift my head from his shoulder and switch back to a more comfortable topic. "FYI, I wasn't taking credit for getting you fired from the museum. I was taking credit for your space party business."

"And why do you get credit for that?" he asks.

My jaw drops open. "Tell me you weren't inspired to start this company after I threw you an adult space party for your twenty-ninth."

"Sweetheart, that was an *orgy*. Otherwise known as the furthest thing from a children's party imaginable."

"Come on, it was an *unintentional* orgy. But whatever. The planetary costumes, though? The cosmic dance breaks? The spherical Earth cakes?" I punch him lightly on the shoulder. "You were inspired, ya jerk."

"Oh! Speaking of orgies." Ralph's voice rises, and the woman across the aisle gives us the stink eye yet again. Ralph clears his throat. "My apologies, ma'am." He turns back to me and whispers, "I forgot to tell you that my mom texted last night. Your parents and my parents went on a double date."

"What? Ew. Oh my God." I bend over and make a retching sound. "Are you telling me our parents had an—"

"No! Sorry. Terrible transition on my part. They just had a few drinks." He pauses. "At least I think that's all they did."

I'm still doubled over.

He places a hand on my back. "Are you okay? Are you really going to throw up?"

I sit up and give him an indignant look. "Dude. That was a faux retch. Don't you know me well enough by now to tell the difference between a faux retch and a real retch?"

He shrugs. "That was a really convincing almost-puke. Not my fault my girl is an amazing writer and an actor too. What a talent."

He kisses me, and I do my best to smile through my nerves.

"Also, there need to be at least five participants to classify it as an orgy," Ralph continues.

"Really?" My nose scrunches. "As a romance writer, I feel like I should already know this information. What's it called when it's a foursome, then?"

"A foursome."

"Okay, yeah, that makes sense." I let out a deep breath. "Ugh. Why are our parents hanging out? How did this even happen? Because, look, no offense, but I really don't want you becoming my stepbrother."

"I don't think that's how that works—"

I wave him off. "I know, I know. Even if our parents fully spouse-swapped and your dad ended up married to my mom, and your mom ended up married to my dad, there would be no blood relation between us, and we'd be free to continue boning as we see fit, but still, that's a little too much togetherness, don't you think? Listen, plenty of readers live and breathe the stepbrother trope! And I totally get it! I went there too in *Stepping on Stegosaurus*. Readers lost their minds when Stego gets blown by Teri, the Pterodactyl, inside that dormant volcano during their parents' wedding. It's one of my most beloved scenes in one of my bestselling books... but not if you ask Janine in Little Rock. Janine in Little Rock hated that scene. Janine in Little Rock one-stars every book of mine she can get her grubby hands on, but everyone else really loved it, and—"

"Cal?" Ralph smooths my hair and looks into my eyes.

"Yeah?" Gosh, I'm breathing heavy. I take a swig of my water.

"You okay?" he asks softly.

"Sure. Yeah. I'm fine."

He brushes his thumb across my cheek. "That scene is awesome. My favorite part is when the volcano erupts at the same time as the stegosaurus. Genius."

"Thank you, Ralph-alpha. Janine in Little Rock said it was completely unrealistic. Which should be a moot point when the dinosaurs wear clothes, get haircuts, and have biker tattoos, but whatever, I stand by my choice and do my research. There was always the possibility that volcano would erupt again. Dormant does not mean extinct. I double-checked with James, and he gave me the Hawaiian stamp of approval."

"I'm sure you did." He smiles at me. "Look, I'm shocked my parents are still together, let alone taking an interest in my life. I assumed their reunion was a fluke, and they'd resume hating each other in a matter of weeks." He shrugs. "But it's been over eighteen months now, and they seem genuinely happy. I guess seeing me so serious about you made them want to get to know your family better." He lifts my chin. "But something tells me this energy coming out of you... it's not about our parents. What's going on?"

He really is the most amazing guy.

Why do I ever hold anything back from him?

"You're right. I'm nervous about this weekend," I say with a sigh.

"What? You?" He gathers me close to him and kisses the top of my head.

"Yeah. Me."

"You'll be great. And I'll be there by your side the entire time."

"Thank you." I snuggle closer to him, my heart feeling all warm and fuzzy. "So you're serious about me, huh?"

"Oh, the serious-est," he rumbles into my hair.

"Serious-est isn't a word, ya dork."

"It is now."

He kisses me slow and deep.

I love this man so damn much.

It's then I realize that everyone around us has settled into their seats.

The sound of light snores wafts through the air.

The aisle is clear.

The little green vacant light on the bathroom is lit.

"You know, in"—I check the time on my phone—"twelve minutes, it will officially be our bone-iversary."

He laughs softly. "You're killing me with that."

"What? Anniversaries are for regular folk. You and me? We get a bone-iversary. And it's time for our induction."

"Our induction? What are you—"

I push him out of his seat until he stands confused in the aisle.

I kneel on his vacated seat, slip a piece of paper in his pocket, and whisper in his ear, "Meet you in the bathroom, baby."

Chapter Two

RALPH

I always thought first-class bathrooms would be roomier than this.

You spend your whole life thinking that everything will be different when you finally get to first class. But it's pretty much the same. The seats are bigger, sure. And the soap in the bathroom is a little fancier. But you're still flying through the sky in a tin can, leaving your very mortal life in someone else's hands.

In this case, my life is in Pat's hands. The pilot's name is Pat. *Pat*. I shook the man's hand on my way onboard. He seemed nice enough, but can I really trust a guy named Pat? A *pat* is a little tap on someone's back when they've done a good job. A pat is a tiny square of butter you spread to smithereens on a slice of toast. Is a man named Pat really up for the challenge of shepherding one hundred and eighty-seven souls through the air and delivering them to safety on the ground below?

That remains to be seen.

Geez, when did I get so judgmental?

I've learned from Calliope that people absolutely do judge a book by its cover. But I know better than to do that to a human being.

You know what? I'm sure Pat is a fantastic pilot. And let's face it, I'm not one to talk when it comes to the power and perception of names, am I? I mean, my name is Ralph. Fucking *Ralph*. A name that did me no favors when I was a twelve-year-old wannabe astronaut at space camp who puked every time he stepped foot in a simulator. Yeah. I was a kid named Ralph who couldn't stop ralphing. Needless to say, that was a long and sorry summer.

Now, here I am all these years later, a grown-ass man flying on an airplane for an anniversary trip with his dream girl.

I should be feeling on top of the world. But instead, it's like I'm being pulled back in time. Back to when I was that scrawny seventh grader who couldn't keep his digestive tract in check.

The plane makes another sudden swerve, and the contents of my stomach lurch with it.

I aim my face toward the toilet bowl, but somehow, I keep it together.

I catch my own eyes in the small mirror over the sink.

"Come on, man," I whisper to my reflection. "You're not that pukey little nerd anymore. You're a confident astronomer with a hot-as-hell girlfriend, and you're doing great things in the world."

Am I, though?

I continue, "Alright, full disclosure? You never became an astronaut like you planned, but you organize really cool kids' birthday parties now, and you narrate your girlfriend's dinosaur love stories on the side."

Christ, when I say it out loud like that, I really want to lose my lunch.

"And you know what? When you narrate her books, you don't even have to be called Ralph anymore. You use a *way* sexier name when you narrate. But that's top secret stuff, my man."

If I get off this aircraft alive, maybe I'll suggest to Pat that he consider a pseudonym. It might give people more immediate confidence in his flying prowess. Maybe... Crew Aerion? That could work. Ooh, or Jupiter Ray?

"Christ, I'm losing my mind in this bathroom!"

With a paper towel in each hand, I steady myself against the plastic walls as another bout of turbulence rocks the aircraft. This is the third one since I've been in here.

After several more minutes of deep breathing, there's a knock on the door.

"Just a minute!" I shout out of habit.

The light knock sounds again.

"I said 'Just a minute!'" I shout even louder, my heart pounding.

"Someone's in here!"

"I know you're in there, Ralpha-alpha," Callie's voice murmurs through the wall. "That's the whole idea."

"Right, right, hi," I say as I unlatch the door.

Calliope squeezes her way in and places her bag down on the small counter next to the sink. She immediately unbuttons her shirt and hoists her breasts higher in her black lace bra. "I know shirt-unbuttoning is discouraged in these situations," she whispers. "Time is of the essence, and it's best to just get in and get out, but I know you like this view, so – oh holy shit, your dick's out!"

"Well, yeah, your note literally said 'Get your dick out, baby. It's time to fly.'"

"So obedient," she purrs and runs her nails down my back. "Did you like my invitation?"

"I did. I do. It's very official. And detailed. Was that pubic hair on the airplane's jet engines?"

She beams. "Yes! My cover designer Janie did it for me! Isn't she amazing? I wanted to create something special for our induction into this most amazing club, and I was brainstorming ideas when it hit me: how have I never noticed the penile potential of an airplane until now? I mean, it's all right there! The main *shaft* of the aircraft? The two round engines dangling below it like balls? Balls literally designed to create *thrust*? Humans have been flying across the planet in sky penises for over a hundred years, and no one's talking about it! So anyway, I shared my vision with Janie, and some strategically placed veins, fleshy tones, and pubic hair later, the official Ralph & Callie Mile High Club logo was born!"

I smile and nod, wondering how the hell I got into this situation.

"So you've been standing here the whole time with your pants down?" She looks impressed.

"Yeah! What took you so long?" I fail to keep the strain out of my voice.

"There was turbulence, dude. Didn't you feel it?"

I consider telling her "Hell yeah, I felt the turbulence! Right down to my nauseous, nerdified soul!" But instead, I say, "Turbulence? Huh. Didn't affect me, I guess."

"Yeah, the announcements to stay seated kept coming, and the friggin' fasten your seat belt sign was pulsing red over my head like a relentless, cockblocking bitch."

"Whoa." I run my hands down her sides.

"Sorry," she says. "You know how I get when I'm excited. So should we do this or what?"

She shimmies her panties down and shoves them into her pocket.

I draw her closer. "You know, we're making a habit of this sex in public thing."

"Oh, I know." She smiles and wraps a leg around my waist.

"You'd think after I lost my job at the museum, I'd be wary of this sort of thing, but—"

"But you can't resist me."

"That I can't." I kiss down her neck.

She nudges me with her hips. "Cool, so put it in."

"Put it in?"

"Sorry, that wasn't exactly sexy pillow talk, but we ain't got no pillows, and we ain't got no time for foreplay, so yeah, put it in."

I hesitate.

"Ralph. Any second now, someone's going to knock on the door. What are you waiting for?"

"I'm just... I'm not quite there yet."

"Oh. Well, let's get you there then." Her voice turns seductive as she slides down to her knees.

I grab her shoulders to pull her back up. "Callie, you don't have to—"

"Stop. You know I worship the ground your penis stands on."

"Aw. That doesn't make sense, but sure, yeah, if you really want to—"

And then she's off and running, so I shut my damn mouth. Because that's what you do when a gorgeous woman wants to go down on you. You shut your mouth and count your blessings.

She's doing that amazing thing where she looks up at me while she works, her eyes all big and beautiful like Bambi.

Bambi? The deer? Where did that image come from?

Who cares.

Just close your eyes and enjoy.

But then, because life is royally screwing with me right now, the plane dips again and I can't stop it this time.

God help me, I can't stop it.

I feel it rise in me, and I try to push her away in time, but I'm not quick enough.

My stomach lurches...

And I puke.

Right on Calliope's adorable, confused forehead.

Oh my God.

Why?

Why, why, why?

She stops what she's doing and pulls away from me.

She touches a finger to her forehead.

For a moment, it's deathly quiet. Except for the overwhelming rumbling airplane sounds rattling the tiny tin can we're attempting to fuck in.

When I speak, my voice sounds hollow in my ears. "Callie. Oh my God. I'm so sorry. I don't know what —"

"You okay?" she asks.

"I guess so, but—"

She stuns the hell out of me with what she says next.

"Then wipe and go."

"What? Are you serious?"

"Wipe and go! We didn't come this far to give up now! Front pocket of my purse! Now!"

I reach into her purse and find a pack of baby wipes. She snatches them from me, wipes her forehead clean, and presses the soiled wipes into the metal trashcan that's part of the wall.

She rises to her feet with renewed energy. "Good to go?" she asks.

This woman is something else.

I clear my throat. "Yeah, um. Good to go, I guess."

"Atta boy," she says.

And we make lift off.

Chapter Three

CALLIOPE

"Ralph. Seriously. Let me carry something."

"Nope. From now on until forever, I carry everything for you."

Our taxi pulls out of the valet semi-circle as we make our way to the hotel entrance. Ralph is a human pack mule. He's wearing not one but two backpacks. He's dragging three full-size suitcases loaded with over a hundred paperback books, and he has my retractable author banner slung across his chest.

"For the hundredth time, Ralph, I'm not mad at you."

"How can you not be, Callie? I puked on your face!"

"Baby, keep your voice down, will you?" I hold the door open for him as he lumbers through with our bags. "Readers are everywhere, and I really try to keep my personal life as private as possible."

When we stop to get our bearings, I manage to wrestle one backpack off him. A small victory. The dark hotel lobby bustles with people in flip-flops, people in ball gowns, and people in pajamas. Apparently, anything goes in Vegas.

"Come here, will you?" He lets me pull him close. "For the last time, Ralph-alpha. You did not puke in my face."

"I did, though!"

"No." I brush my cheek along his stubble as I search for the right words. "You... coated my forehead with a surprise that I didn't see coming."

"Come on," he scoffs, but he smiles, and I feel him responding to my touch like he always does.

"*And*," I continue. "You were gentlemanly enough to avoid my hair, which was impressive and always greatly appreciated. Then, like a real champ, you rallied your spirits—and your queasy stomach—to officially usher us into the Mile High Club. Believe me when I say I have zero complaints."

"You do realize you still smell like puke," he murmurs into my neck.

"I do, yeah. Let's check in so we can shower as soon as humanly possible."

I grab a suitcase from him and roll toward the welcome desk, where several people are ahead of us in line.

"You know," I whisper to him as we settle in line. "At first, I wasn't sure what the hell had happened. Because that wasn't the first time you've coated my face with a *surprise*, so I assumed it was *that* kind of surprise, which you know I wholeheartedly welcome. But then I realized no, your dick was in my mouth, so how could it also explode on my face? And besides, you never come that quickly and—"

"Callie? Can we table this discussion for later? Please?"

"Sure. Why are you so tense all of a sudden?"

He leans closer to me. "What happened to 'I keep my personal life as private as possible?' That woman is definitely listening in on our conversation."

"What woman?" I say way too loudly and whip my head around.

A tall woman with curly blond hair and red glasses beams at us next to Ralph. She's wearing a T-shirt that says "I Like Big Books and I Cannot Lie."

"Hi!" she squeals. "Ohmygosh hi! I'm Jane! Sorry to be all eavesdroppy and nosy, but I would recognize that voice anywhere!"

I smile back at her. "That's okay. Hi. I'm Tracy Triassic." I reach out and shake her hand. "Are you one of my readers?"

"Yes, I am, but I wasn't actually..."

It's then that I realize her focus isn't on me.

At all.

She's staring at Ralph.

"Rock? Rock Cosmos, is that you?" she says with wide-eyed

wonder.

Ralph is checking a text and doesn't fully register the woman's words. "Whoa, speaking of rocks! Callie, look! Wally bought a ring!" He holds his phone up to me, displaying a photo of a gorgeous diamond ring in a small wooden box. "Mabel doesn't know, though. Wally said we're sworn to secrecy."

I do my best to keep a smile plastered to my face when I say, "Wow, maybe we should talk about that later, *Rock*. Jane here wants to say hi to you."

His eyebrows scrunch together. "Rock? Why are you calling me...?"

I nudge him and take my smile up a notch.

He finally looks at Jane, who bounces on her toes in excitement at this point. I watch the light bulb go on. "Ohhhhhh. Rock! Yes, I'm Rock Cosmos. Nice to meet you, Jane."

He shakes her hand, and she shivers in delight.

She honest to God shivers.

"This is amazing!" she yells. "I listened to all ten books you've narrated in one week! All day, every day! I just couldn't stop myself! In the car. In the kitchen. In the garage. In the shower. In the bedroom. On the toilet—"

"Wow!" I interrupt. "That's a lot of listening. Thanks so much for—"

She ignores me. "Sign my boob, Rock. Can you please sign my boob?"

In a flash, the woman has her T-shirt neck pulled down, her right breast propped up, and a permanent blue marker whipped out.

When Ralph and I first decided to try out this partnership as author and narrator, we knew he'd need a pseudonym. Don't get me wrong, I think the name Ralph is sexy as hell, but I'm a smart businesswoman too, and that name just wouldn't fly in the romance sphere. Also, I already cost him his job at the museum, so I didn't want to be responsible for Ralph losing another work opportunity. Romance is the highest-selling genre in the book industry, so clearly, millions of people read it, but disrespect and judgment still run rampant. All it would take is one of the space birthday parents whispering to her friends that wholesome party planner Ralph Anderson narrates porn and… poof! His new business would go up in smoke.

We couldn't risk that, so Rock Cosmos was born.

Was it my favorite choice for a pseudonym? No. My vote was for Orion Kuiperbelt, which I thought was kitschy and cool, but I was shot down on that one.

Ralph takes the marker from Jane and looks at me for… something. Advice? Permission?

"Go on, Rock," I say with a laugh. "Sign the woman's boob already."

So he does. My boyfriend very gently presses a Sharpie into a stranger's bosom and signs his pseudonym across her flesh.

I can't be certain, but I think she orgasms right there in front of us.

When he finishes, he caps the marker and hands it back to her. "There ya go, Jane. See you at the signing tomorrow?"

"Oh you bet you will! Thank you! Thank you so much!" Ralph's fangirl gives him a happy, squealy hug, then runs to the elevator, clutching her hand to her breast, not looking back at me once.

Huh. I guess I was so nervous about this signing, wondering how I would be perceived as a writer, that it didn't even occur to me my assistant might have his own fans.

But this is good, right? It means the audio is doing well and listeners are enjoying it.

I should be happy.

So why do I have this tight feeling in my stomach?

"Callie? Cal? Calliope?"

"What's up? What?" I startle out of my thoughts.

"They're ready for us," Ralph places a hand on my lower back and nods at the hotel clerk, who waits with a friendly smile.

I go through all the motions of checking in, but suddenly, all I really want to do is go home.

Chapter Four

RALPH

*C*allie made a beeline for the bathroom as soon as we walked into our hotel suite. I offered to join her, but she insisted on showering alone.

I could have let that bruise my already fragile ego, but it's fine.

She's nervous about tomorrow.

And probably needs some space.

I'm a wise enough man to give it to her.

I'm lying on the bed, soaking in the over-the-top Vegas-ness of it all, when the water shuts off in the next room.

"Hey! A heart-shaped bed?" I shout. "That spins? And a mirrored ceiling? Baby, this is amazing. Ridiculous but amazing!"

"I'm glad you like it," Calliope enters the room wrapped in a white towel and heads straight for our temporary closet, which is also mirrored.

Seriously, this suite has so many mirrors.

She slides a fluffy pink bathrobe off a hanger and slips it around her shoulders.

I hop onto all fours on the bed and reach for the little red light above the headboard. "Dare me to press the button?"

"Go for it," she says.

I press it. The bed spins me around and around at warp speed.

"Holy shit!" I yelp and grip the mattress to keep from going airborne.

"Hahaha, oh my God!" Calliope laughs at my expense.

"Can this be right?!" I shout. "There's gotta be a slower gear on this, doesn't there?"

"You'd think!" She laughs some more. "Unless this is the sort of thing people are into these days? Can you imagine trying to get something going while you're spinning like that?"

"Get something going? You mean, like this?" I pump my hips into the mattress and make exaggerated sounds of passion. "Ugh! Mmm! Oh yeah. That's it! Right there!"

Yeah, I'm acting like an idiot, but she's laughing again. That's a good enough reason for me to continue.

"Get on here with me, woman!" I yell. "Wheeeee!"

"I'm good watching you from here, thanks!"

She's doubled over with laughter now.

"You sure?" I get back on my knees and pretend to swing a lasso over my head. "Wheeeeeeeeeee!"

Suddenly, I feel like a little kid on Christmas morning. Scratch that. I'm Jewish, so Christmas mornings were just like any other morning. And little kids don't spin on beds in Vegas hotels with their hot author girlfriends, but you get the idea.

I'm excited to be here.

I feel possibility here.

And I haven't felt that in a while.

Meeting that listener in line earlier gave me a boost I think I needed. It made me feel like maybe I am on a path to something good and worthwhile. Perhaps I've stumbled into doing something meaningful for others. Or at least to that one lady.

"Careful you don't puke again, Anderson!" Calliope winks, then pads up the tiny flight of stairs leading to an epic wall-to-wall, floor-to-ceiling window.

"You're right. You're right." I press the button a second time, and the bed jerks to a stop. It takes a moment for the dizziness to pass, but thankfully, the queasiness doesn't rear its head again.

Calliope stares out at the view, her back to me.

I swing my legs over the side of the bed and walk up the steps to join her. Wrapping my arms around her from behind, I bring her back to my front.

"Mmm. You smell good," I say.

"Better than puke?" She chuckles.

"Oh yeah, baby. Way better than puke."

She still feels tense in my arms.

"Can you believe this view?" I plant a kiss on her cheek. "The Eiffel Tower in the middle of the desert? How cool is that?"

"Really cool," she murmurs.

The golden lights on the tower sparkle in a minute-long light show.

When it ends, I say, "Hey. Remember that scene in *Rain Man* where Charlie Babbit and Raymond slow dance in that big-ass window overlooking Vegas?"

"How could I forget? Best moment of the movie."

I turn her around to face me and sway with her in my arms. "Look. Now that's us."

She smiles as we dance. "If you're using a *Rain Man* reference to seduce me, you're losing your touch, Anderson."

"In my defense, it's not often that I *have* to seduce you. You're usually ready to go."

"Yeah, well, I'm not a sex robot." She exhales. "I can't just turn it on when I'm not feeling it."

"So I did upset you earlier, huh? With the whole signing of the boob thing? Because listen, I was thinking, if the situation were reversed and a male reader took out his penis for you to sign, and you signed it, I probably wouldn't have handled that so well."

"That would never happen."

"Random men don't pull out their penises?" I say hopefully.

"Oh no, random men pull out their penises all the time. Just not at book events."

"Oh." My eyebrows pull together.

She runs her thumb down the center of my forehead and smooths out the creases there, something she always does when she catches me overthinking.

She continues massaging that spot while she speaks. "First of all, very few male readers attend romance signings. And the ones who do attend are usually there to support their lady. Help her get good spots in line, carry her books, that sort of thing. Pulling out a penis would be a surefire way to get ousted. And arrested."

I guide her hand away from my face and lead her into a spin as we continue to slow dance.

"Well, that's quite the double standard, isn't it? A woman can take out her breast, and it's no problem, but God forbid a penis appears on the scene and—"

"I'm gonna stop you right there, sir. You're not about to argue the point that women have it easier than men, are you?"

Mouth, insert foot.

I put my hands up. "No way. Would never."

"And you're not actively advocating for open-air penis time for all, are you?" she asks.

Looks like we're definitely done dancing.

"Nope." I shake my head vigorously. "Open-air penis time for all sounds pretty problematic. Though it could be a catchy T-shirt slogan for your nudist friend Mabel maybe?"

"Yeah, maybe." Calliope half laughs, then plops down on a velvet bench by the window. "So Wally's going to propose, huh?"

She resumes gazing out at the city.

"He is." I take a seat beside her and place a hand on her thigh.

She sighs. "That's... good. I'm sure that will make Mabel really happy."

She's hard to read right now.

Hesitantly, I say, "Does that information make *you* feel any certain way?"

"Society's relationship to breasts is bonkers!" She startles me with the change in subject. "I mean, look at that billboard over there. You see it?"

She points at a massive billboard of a bikini-clad woman.

"I see it, yeah."

"It's cleavage city, right? Upperboob! Underboob! Sideboob! It's all there! Except of course for the sneaky naughty little nipple hiding under that tiny triangle of fabric, but more on that in a minute. That woman is selling cigars. Cigars! There's no reason for her to be in a string bikini. But advertisers will use every available inch of the breast they can to sell products. And that's totally fine! Because it serves them. But if that same woman needs to breastfeed her child on a park bench, those same white-haired suits who paid for the billboard will be outraged at her audacity. They'll tell her to 'have some respect.' To 'cover up.' And Lord help us all if there is a nip slip on that park bench. The female nipple needs to stay covered at all costs! Which is so freaking weird when you really think about it. Men flaunt their useless nipples whenever and wherever they please! We all have nipples! The nipple is universal! It's one thing that connects us all!"

She's flushed and out of breath. She suddenly looks so young. So innocent.

"Can I give you a hug?" I ask.

"Yeah, I think I need one."

I wrap my arms around her and pull her close. She gives her weight over to me.

"The nipple is the one thing that connects us all, huh?" I chuckle.

"Shut up," she murmurs into my shoulder.

"Can I tell you something I've noticed during the amazing two years we've been together?" I say after a few moments of silence.

"That I'm an amazing woman, and you want to be with me forever?"

"Absolutely that, yes." I kiss the top of her head. "And also... *sometimes*... when you're upset about something specific, you rail against something very broad. For example, right now, I have a hunch you're pissed at me for signing that woman's chest. But instead of telling me that outright, you gave me a rousing speech about the state of breast and nipple rights in our country."

"Oh, you know me so well now, do ya?" She gives me a playful shove.

"I do. I mean, I hope I do." I take her hand and lead her down the steps to our heart-shaped bed. I lie back on the red comforter and pat the space beside me. "Come here."

She curls up in the little spoon position.

"Sorry I'm out of sorts," she says.

"Nothing to be sorry for." I nibble her ear. "It would be helpful, though, if you leveled with me a bit more sometimes. I know I'm a pretty evolved creature as far as men go, but once in a while, I can be a dumb guy just like the rest of them."

We're silent for a moment as a noisy group of partygoers makes their way down the hall outside our room.

Finally, she says, "I'm not upset that you signed that woman's breast. I was just surprised, I guess? And I think the news about Wally and Mabel is great. Super happy for them. Again, I think I'm just... surprised." She sighs. "Do you ever feel like life keeps surprising you, and all your plans and ambitions and expectations keep changing on you, and you sometimes don't know who you are anymore or how to make sense of it all or keep up with the world around you?"

"All the time."

"Really?" She rolls onto her back to look at me.

"Really." I cup her cheek and let my thumb stroke back and forth a few times. "Want to hear something I *do* know?"

"What's that?"

"Tomorrow is going to be great. You're an incredible writer with wonderful fans. You have nothing to worry about. Remember the musical montage moment in *Rain Man* when they ride down the casino escalator in those matching tan suits looking all suave and ready to win big? That'll be us tomorrow."

"Are we going to wear matching suits?" She smirks.

"No." I smile and kiss her on the forehead. "But we're gonna win big."

"Thanks, baby. I don't deserve you."

"Yeah, you do."

She snuggles into my chest and sighs. "Mmm. You're my cinnamon roll."

"Excuse me? Your what?"

"You've heard me talk about cinnamon rolls in romance, haven't you?"

"I don't think I have, no."

She pulls back slightly and cups my cheeks. "You're ooey gooey on the inside."

"That's a good thing, right?"

"Hell yeah! It's a great thing. The cinnamon roll guy is sensitive and kind. He's sort of the antidote to all the angsty asshole guys so many authors write about. I write them too. Kent in *Kentrosaurus' Keeper* and Barry in *Bootycalling the Baryonyx* were real dicks. Those kinds of guys are awesome for fiction. But in real life?

Gimme my cinnamon roll."

"This isn't your sly way of telling me I'm getting doughy, is it?" I ask.

"No, ya dork. You're the sexiest, most chiseled pastry I've ever seen. You're a rock-hard cinnamon roll. With abs."

"So I'm a day-old discounted cinnamon roll is what you're getting at," I say, tickling her.

Her laughter bounces through the room.

The best sound in the world.

"Shut up and kiss me, will you?" she whispers.

"Don't mind if I do."

Chapter Five

CALLIOPE

"*T*racy, is that you?" A goddess of a woman in a flowing gold dress approaches my table while Ralph and I are setting up.

"Oh my God, it's Joella Flanders," I hiss to him. "Joella Flanders is saying hi to me."

Ralph smiles at the woman and says out of the corner of his mouth, "You know she can hear you, right?" He nudges me, then continues arranging the books.

"Joella!" I snap out of my awe-induced stupor and reach out to shake her hand across the table.

"What's this hand-shaking baloney?" she says. "Come here and gimme a hug, girl!"

I shimmy out from behind our display and get pulled right into her sequin-covered arms.

They're itchy, but I don't care. This is Joella freaking Flanders we're talking about.

"It's so great to finally see you in real life!" I say into her sparkly bosom. "I wasn't sure you'd recognize me from my little square on social media."

She releases me from the hug. "Come on, now. I'd know you anywhere. Don't let anyone tell you that internet book friends aren't real friends. They're the best friends!"

I step back to stare up at her gorgeous six-foot two frame. "Sure, but you're... *you!*"

Joella Flanders is an absolute powerhouse in the industry. She organized this entire event. She had six books on the *New York Times* Bestseller list at the same time for over eight weeks.

Last year she sold more books than the Bible. And to top it all off, she's an awesome generous person who everyone wants to be around.

She waves off my adoration. "And you're you, honey! I've been so delighted watching your career climb these past few years. You're doing it, baby!"

"Eh," I say.

"What's that? What's 'eh'?" She mimics my voice and my shrug.

"I don't know if I'd really call it a climb. More like a... herky-jerky bounce. I've been up and down and all around lately. But listen, I don't want to sound ungrateful. Thank you again so much for that back cover quote you wrote for me last year. I know that was the reason so many new readers took a chance on me."

"They took a chance on you because you're a great writer."

"Tell that to Janine from Little Rock," I say under my breath.

"What's that?"

"Nothing." I smile. "Seriously, Joella, thank you for all you do. The book world is lucky to have you."

A group of authors across the aisle squeals as they reunite and hug one another.

I watch them a moment.

"You okay, kiddo?" Joella places a ring-covered hand on my shoulder.

"I'm fine, yeah!"

She cocks her head to the side like she doesn't quite believe me.

Just then, an announcement comes over the speakers. "Alright authors, the doors will be opening in two minutes. Two minutes!"

I feel my heart rate spike.

"Oh, I didn't say hi to your beau!" She jogs her way over to Ralph and shakes his hand. "Sorry to be rude. I'm Joella."

"Pleasure to meet you," he says. "I'm Ralph. I've heard such great things about you."

"How did you know he's my beau? He could have just been my assistant." I immediately realize how terrible that sounds. I lock eyes with Ralph. "Not *just* my assistant. I didn't mean it like that. I just meant that—"

Joella pulls me aside and whispers in my ear, "Just an assistant wouldn't look at an author the way that boy looks at you."

She moves toward her corner of the signing space where mountains of books are displayed, three assistants ready to support her, and at least sixty feet of velvet rope winding back and forth to create a corral for her inevitable hordes of fans. Before she gets too far away, she turns and says, "Find me again before all this madness is over, Trace. I think I've been where you're at. We'll talk."

"Thank you, Joella. That's really..."

Did my voice crack just now?

I clear my throat. "Happy signing!"

"Happy signing, you." She winks and takes her place.

I return to Ralph and kiss him on the cheek. "Sorry about the 'just my assistant' thing."

He waves a hand. "I totally get it. She calls you Trace, huh?"

"Yeah. I should have mentioned that. These events get a little wonky with real names and pen names flying around. So it's best to just assume everyone wants you to use their pseudonym."

"I should call you Tracy too then?"

"Sure. Why not."

"Kinky." He grabs a handful of my ass. "I like it."

I give him a playful slap. "Hands off the merchandise, mister."

"Speaking of merchandise..." He gestures to our table full of paperbacks, pins, and bookmarks. "What am I supposed to do with all this?"

"Damn, I should have given you a run-down of how everything works last night. I was a little distracted."

"I'm not complaining. You gave me a run-down of a different kind." He lifts his brows twice.

I roll my eyes. "You're such a cheeseball."

"Wait. Am I a cheeseball or a cinnamon roll?" He gathers me in his arms.

"Both," I say. "Definitely both."

"Ooh, can I be one of those cheesy buns from Red Lobster? Everybody loves those."

"Everybody loves *you.*" I run my hands through his shaggy

chocolate-brown hair. "*I* love you. Thank you for being here with me."

"Love you too, baby. Nowhere else I'd rather be."

We kiss.

Then I'm back in business mode.

"Basically, smile at people, hand me the books I need to sign, help me put them in the cute baggies with stickers, and ask folks to sign up for my newsletter if they're not subscribed already."

"I can do that."

"Great." I do a little jump and shake my nerves out. "Okay, how much time do we have left?"

The announcement sounds over the speaker again. "Thirty seconds, everyone!"

"Thirty seconds," Ralph repeats with a smile.

The announcer continues, "And a reminder to all attendees. Once we open the doors, there is to be no stampeding. I repeat, no stampeding."

Ralph's smile drops. "Geezuz, did she just say no *stampeding*?"

"Yeah, but don't worry about that. We won't get a stampede. We'll be lucky if we get a trickle."

Famous last words.

Because a few moments later, the doors open, and we don't get a trickle.

We get a stampede.

But the stampede is not for me.

Chapter Six

RALPH

"Damn, my hand is cramping up. Is your hand cramping up?" I say to Calliope as I sign what must be the hundredth book in the past hour. I've also been signing tote bags, coffee mugs, wall canvases, panties, and a variety of female body parts. Apparently, we've moved beyond the boob. Today, I've signed shoulder blades, hip bones, and lower backs too. One lady even asked me to sign her foot.

This must be what rock stars feel like.

When Calliope asked me to assist her this weekend, I was not expecting this. I thought I'd be sitting here, proudly supporting my girl and watching her do her thing. But it turns out, I have fans too.

Jane from yesterday told one person I was here in the flesh, that person told another person, and boom!

Rock Cosmos is an audio sensation.

They've been listening, and they love what they're hearing.

The best part of it is that Calliope and I are officially a team now.

A partnership.

That's an amazing feeling.

I hand the signed book to our last listener in line. She clutches it to her chest and squeals as she walks away.

A final bell rings, and the announcer's voice comes over the loudspeaker. "That signals the end of Signing Session A. Everyone from Signing Session A wearing a lavender wristband should be exiting the room. Authors, Session B will begin in just ten minutes! Take a few minutes to stretch, breathe, visit the restroom, and get ready for another round of mayhem! Session B starts in ten minutes!"

"Whew! This is wild, isn't it?" I stand and stretch my arms overhead.

"Wild, yeah," Calliope says as she reorganizes her Tracy Triassic stickers and merchandise.

I wrap my arms around her and give her a happy squeeze. "You've been holding out on me, madam. Why didn't you tell me Rock Cosmos is an audio sensation?"

She stiffens. "Did you really just call yourself an audio sensation, Ralph?"

"No. I called *Rock Cosmos* an audio sensation. Ralph is but Rock's humble servant, bringing his growly, sexy tones to the altar of Tracy Triassic fans in service of tantalizing their earholes."

Her nose wrinkles. "Earholes? Gross, dude."

"Yeah, that was pretty gross. Sorry. Apparently, I'm good at *saying* words. But I never claimed to be good at *writing* them. How about we leave that part to you?"

"Sounds good, because I promise you, no one wants you to tantalize their earholes."

"You sure about that?" I flash a little pink rectangle at her. "That Roseanna Halbrook author lady gave me her card. Said her readers have been asking her to hire me."

"Oh." Her face falls.

"What?"

"So... you're going to narrate for other authors now?"

"I'm not sure. Maybe? Would that be okay with you?

"Sure! Of course, that's okay with me!"

"Are you sure? Because your voice is really squeaky right now."

"*Your* voice is squeaky right now!" she fires back.

It's moments like this that I remember Calliope didn't grow up in a house with the healthiest communication. But in all fairness, who did?

"Oh, wait," she continues. "Your voice isn't squeaky. It's 'deep, dark and delicious. An orgasm on toast,' right? Is that what that reader said when she had you sign her lunchbox?" She scoffs.

"Who brings a lunchbox to a book signing, and what the hell is an 'orgasm on toast'?"

I consider making a joke about breakfast in bed but decide this is probably not the right moment for that. I place my hands gently on her shoulders and let them slide down her arms instead.

"Callie, if you don't want me to work for other authors, I won't."

She sighs and puts her head in her hands, like she's hiding from me. "No, it's fine. What am I, Ursula in *The Little Mermaid*? I don't own your voice or anything."

"Hey," I say softly. "Could you look at me maybe?"

She drops her hands and looks up at me. "I guess I thought this whole narration thing would be – I dunno – our thing. It feels kind of intimate you doing that with someone else."

"To be clear, I wouldn't be *sleeping* with anyone else. Just reading their sexy books. Out loud. For money."

She laughs. "See? When you say it like that, it sounds all sorts of wrong!"

I scan the room full of authors, books, and banners and remember the excitement of the past few hours.

"Did you see all those people? The way they responded to me?" I ask.

"I did. I saw."

I shrug. "It seems like maybe I'm decent at this."

"You're awesome at this," she sighs then shakes her head like she's getting rid of a thought she doesn't want to be thinking. "You should absolutely narrate for other authors." She pauses and smiles. "Just don't forget where you got your start, huh?"

"Forget where I got my start?" I chuckle. "Callie, how could—"

Joella Flanders rushes up to us before I can fully respond.

"Whoooey!" She wipes a bead of sweat from her lip. "You two had quite the line in your neck of the woods, didn't you!"

"We were busy, yeah!" Calliope says.

Joella is out of breath and scanning the room. "Super happy for you both of course, but listen, we're having spacing issues. There were a whole bunch of giant clusterfucks jamming up the aisles that we weren't expecting. I have crews in here right now taping out a better path for some of the queues, but in the meantime, can I ask a favor of you two?

"Of course," Calliope says. "Anything for you."

"We'd love it if Stone here..." She gestures to me.

"It's Rock actually," I say proudly.

"Ah, sorry about that. We'd love if *Rock* here could do an impromptu live read for us? Attendees are apparently all a twitter about him being here, and we think it would be a great way to entertain folks while they wait in these long lines. We could bring over a little raised platform and a microphone for behind your table? Then you can let 'er rip right from there? Maybe read some of your favorite scenes from Tracy's books for us?"

"Oh, I don't think—"

Calliope starts to speak just as I say, "Bring it on, baby!!"

"Amazing!" Joella places a grateful hand on her heart. "Thank you both so much!"

She snaps her fingers as she hurries down the aisle. A crew of men in black pants and glittery T-shirts appear out of nowhere and start assembling a platform behind our book display.

"Bring it on, baby?" Calliope whispers to me.

"Yeah. I don't know where that came from either," I whisper back. "This place is doing things to me."

The announcement speaker clicks on again. "Authors, this is your two-minute warning. Doors for Session B will open in two minutes."

"Which book do you think I should read from?" I scan the over twenty titles we have displayed on the table.

"Um. I dunno, Ralph. This feels a little—"

"Didn't you say we're supposed to address each other by our pseudonyms while we're here, Tracy?" I pat her on the butt and give her some Rock Cosmos sass.

"I did, yeah."

"Then call me Rock, sexpot. Ooh!" I grab a book from the stack. "You mentioned the volcano scene from *Stepping on Stegosaurus* before. Let's do that one! That scene really packs a punch."

I start flipping through the book to find the right chapter just as one of the crew guys motions me over to test out the microphone.

"Wish me luck, babe." I give her a quick kiss on the cheek and hustle up to the microphone. "Testing, testing, 1, 2, 3. I've always wanted to say that," I joke with the crew guys.

When the thirty-second warning comes over the loudspeaker, I undo the top few buttons on my shirt and roll up the sleeves to my forearms. If I've learned anything from narrating Calliope's books, it's that ladies love shirtsleeves rolled up to a guy's forearms.

"Go, team!" I shout to Callie down at the table, but either she doesn't hear me, or she ignores me.

The doors open for Session B, and the room instantly floods with readers.

Joella sidles up beside me and speaks into the microphone. "Welcome to all our newbies! And welcome back to those of you who are double dipping today, you lucky pups, you! As many of you heard – and some of you experienced – we had longer wait times than anticipated at our first session, so to make this round more enjoyable, we have a surprise aural treat for you. Allow me to introduce you to Roid Universe – "

"It's Rock Cosmos, actually," I gently correct.

"My apologies. Rock Cosmos! He has generously offered to live narrate some spicy scenes for us while we wait in line today. Take it away, Rock!"

"I love you, Rock!" a woman shouts from the crowd.

"Oh wow. I... love you too. And thank you for that lovely introduction, Joella. We'll kick things off today with an excerpt from Tracy Triassic's *Stepping on Stegosaurus*, an enemies-to-lovers stepbrother romance. For dinosaurs."

A hush falls over the crowd. For a moment, all I can hear is the sound of my own breathing.

Then I launch into the scene, my new narration voice in full effect.

"'Raaaaah!' Teri caws as she soars into the dark cavern of the volcano, her pterodactyl wings spreading wide, her labia following suit. The plates of armor that run a skyward path along my spine—the calling card of the stegosaurus—stand as erect as ever, perhaps even more so now that my desired and forbidden mate has entered the building. 'Are you sure this volcano is dormant?' she asks. Her voice instantly affects me. Like it always does. My stepsister. My nemesis. My lover. My everything. 'That's what I was told,' I say. 'Seems you were told wrong, stepbrother,' she responds with that sass I can never resist. 'See that red-hot lava brewing by your feet? Seems you're not the only thing that's about to blow.' With that, she knocks me on my side, opens her beak wide and goes to town on my twelve-foot dino dick."

I look up from the pages to gauge the response of the room.

"Don't stop!" a woman with a rainbow tutu shouts. "Don't ever stop!"

"What she said!" a lady dressed in a leather corset adds.

I dive back into the text.

"The lava burns, but not as hot as my desire for her. 'Most women with a beak this long would have trouble finding the right suction, but not you, Teri. Your beak feels like lips, and your sandpaper tongue feels like heaven.'"

"Sexy, sexy, sexy!" a lady gasps in the aisle and fans herself with a paperback.

"Take it off!" a woman wearing a unicorn horn shouts from over thirty feet away.

She whips her own bra off and slingshots it across the space. It soars through the air like a mint-green meteor.

I catch it with my teeth.

At that moment, an aspect of my personality that had been dormant inside me ignites.

And I lose my damn mind.

I gnash at the bra like an animal before letting it fall to my feet.

Tearing off my shirt, I toss it into the crowd.

Pops and thrusts from my crotch accompany the words that come out of my mouth.

If I could get down on this platform and perform the worm while still handling the mic, I would.

I am a passionate prehistoric one-man show.

"'The lava's rising, baby. We gotta get out,' I say, panic in my throat. 'Not a chance, stepbrother,' Teri says. 'Not before we get *off*.' God, I love this winged woman. Her priorities are impeccable. 'You know what I discovered yesterday, Stego?' she continues.

'I'm not actually a dinosaur.' 'Oh no?' I pant. 'No. Pterodactyls are flying reptiles, aka distant dinosaur cousins.' She puts her beak back on me, and I nearly pass out from the pleasure. 'Sister. Cousin,' I say. 'It all works for me.'"

This is one of the many things I love about Calliope's writing. She keeps it sexy but always finds a way to educate her readers as well.

"My orgasm looms bigger and brighter on the horizon as the lava raises us higher and higher. My spiky tail is burnt. The tips of her wings are singed, but neither of us gives a fuck because we're—"

I break character and send my regular Ralph voice into the microphone.

"Sorry, everyone, am I allowed to say the word fuck in here?"

"Fuck yeah, you are!" a chorus of female voices shouts back.

I flash them the Rock Cosmos smile. "Well then, let's fucking continue."

They cheer.

I didn't even know I had a Rock Cosmos smile, but apparently, I do.

I return to the page to bring them the story climax they're clearly craving.

"... but neither of us gives a fuck because we're in love. I may be the length of a bus with a brain the size of a walnut, but my heart is the exact right size. I'm in love with my nemesis-stepsister-cousin, and I don't care if the whole world knows it. So for the first time ever, I say it out loud. 'I love you, Teri.' She lifts her pointy head and focuses those beautiful beady eyes on me. 'I love you too, Steggo. Let's fly, baby.' With one last whip of her wing across my thing, the volcano erupts at the same moment my dino dick does. We're shot up to the sky, spurts of lava and stegosaurus seed spewing as far as the eye can see. It's bliss and terror. Exhilaration and wonder. It's love."

I close the book to thunderous applause.

And a very angry girlfriend.

When I step off the platform, Calliope stands behind her retractable banner, staring at the wall.

"What are you doing?" I whisper. "It's time to sell some books, baby!"

"Seems like you've got that covered," she says, still avoiding my eyes.

"What's going on with you? I thought you'd be happy. We're making a splash here!"

"No, *you're* making a splash here."

"Highlighting *your* books! Remember that scene in *Rain Man*? Dustin Hoffman's character is the one who counts the cards, but Tom Cruise's character still reaps the benefit of that! They're a team. We're a team!"

"Okay, you've got to stop with the *Rain Man* stuff! *Rain Man* cannot be the only Vegas movie you're capable of referencing." She takes in what is surely a blank look on my face. "Oh my God, *is* it?"

"Well, I can't think of any others at the moment..."

"*The Godfather, Swingers, Ocean's 11, Pay it Forward, Mars Attacks!, The Hangover, Paul Blart: Mall Cop 2*. Take your pick, dude!"

"I'm a former astronomer, Calliope, and now a little kid party planner and erotic narrator, not a movie critic! How many skills does a guy gotta have before you deem him acceptable?"

"What the hell does that mean? I find you acceptable! I find you more than acceptable. I'm crazy about you, you idiot!"

I shrug. "Certainly doesn't feel that way right now."

"Wait a damn second. You just totally stole this experience out from under me, but I'm the bad guy? You made me feel like—"

"Come on, Callie." I interrupt her. "No one can make you feel a certain way. That's Emotional Intelligence 101. If you're feeling unseen or unappreciated, that's on you."

Her mouth drops open, but she doesn't say a thing.

I peek out from behind the banner at the long line of readers assembled.

Shit. That was mean.

I should apologize.

But instead, I sigh and say, "Can we table this for now and just be a team?"

She doesn't answer me.

"Come on, baby. A ton of people are waiting on us."

"You know what, Ralph? I take it back. You're not a cinnamon roll. You're a jerk."

She gathers her sweater and purse and squeezes out from behind our display.

"Where are you going?" I whisper-shout.

She gives me a little bow. "The table's all yours, Rock. Enjoy."

Before I can say anything else, she disappears into the crowd.

Chapter Seven

CALLIOPE

I've never been one for gambling.

My family used to take trips to Atlantic City when I was a kid. The beach was fun, but whenever we walked through the casinos, I felt this weird wave of melancholy wash over me. Even as a kid, I knew it wasn't The People's Playground or whatever the TV commercials always said it was. All I saw were lots of bleary-eyed grown-ups staring at slot machines, looking sad and smoking cigarettes.

So hunkering down in front of a Vegas slot machine right now seems like the perfect place to throw myself a pity party.

I prop my phone on the ledge under the sparkling silver words "Crazy Diamonds" and dial up my two besties for our weekly video call. I pop a quarter into the machine while I wait for them to connect. As I watch the slots spin and not line up, I think about how crazy it is that one of the women I'm calling is getting a diamond of her own soon.

Louise pops on the screen with a surprised look on her face. "Hey, sister friend. I thought it was just Mabel and me today. Aren't you supposed to be in the middle of signing? Where's Ralph?"

"It's a long story. Are we all assembled?"

"Almost," she says. "Looks like Mabel's here, but her video isn't on yet."

"I'm here, I'm here!" our sweet friend chirps through the audio, then appears on camera.

Topless.

And presumably bottomless.

"Mabel!" Louise and I shout in unison.

Mabel sits proudly in her living room until realization dawns. "Oh, sorry! I forgot to put on a robe. Want me to get one?" She gestures to a pale-green silk robe on a hook behind her.

"Yes, please," Louise says diplomatically.

Mabel shoots to her feet, and her little square fills with the fleshy evidence that she is, in fact, bottomless as well.

"Alright, guys, I'm going audio only for this one!" Louise says and shuts off her video.

"Hey, Mabes?" I say tentatively. "I thought you put a pause on the nudist lifestyle?"

"A pause?" She stretches the word pause into three syllables and drapes the robe over her shoulders. "Turns out beekeeping and nudity don't mix, so have to choose my moments more judiciously. But, no. You don't ever press pause on the nudist lifestyle. Not once you get a taste of this kind of freeeeeeeedom!"

She accompanies the word freedom with an exuberant shoulder shimmy that keeps giving and giving.

"You gonna close that robe or what?" I avert my eyes.

"Yup! Cinching as we speak." Mabel wraps her robe tight and ties the sash. "Louise, I'm cinched. Please come back."

"Nope." Louise's voice comes through the phone, but still no image. "We have Iris with us this weekend. I can't risk an almost eight-year-old seeing you in all your freeeeeeedom."

"I promise I'll be clothed for the rest of this call," Mabel says. "But just curious, what is the harm in Iris seeing the female form? Won't she be in the room with you when you give birth? Because if so, that experience will be nudity on full blast! I hear a lot of women poop too when they're pushing and—"

"Mabes," I scold. "Come on."

"Yeah, you're right. That was too much. Sorry, Lou, I'm just really excited for you!" Mabel gives a little squeal.

Louise responds, "To answer your question, Mabel, hell no. Iris will not be in the room when I give birth. I'm not sure I'm even letting James in the room for that."

Louise just told us last week that she and James are expecting a baby. Total surprise. For them. For us. For everyone.

I can't figure out if she's happy about it or not.

"How're you feeling, Lou?" I ask.

"Fine, I guess? The nausea's passed, thank God. But I'm only three months, so I'm not showing yet. James is beyond excited, though. Now that we're out of the first trimester, he's telling everyone who'll listen that we're pregnant."

"*We're* pregnant?" I scoff. "Typical guy."

"What do you mean?" Louise asks.

"I hate when guys say *we're* pregnant. No, *she's* pregnant. You got her pregnant. By doing the fun part. How is there not more outrage about that?"

"More outrage about what?"

"That literally all the guy needs to do is have some sex, and then the woman takes care of all the hard stuff! But as I said, it's typical. Guys always swoop in for the fun stuff and take credit for women's hard work."

"Calliope, what's up?" Louise's voice turns serious.

She clicks her video back on.

"Yeah," Mabel's head tilts to the side. "Are you actually mad that James is happy about being a dad again?"

I sigh. "Well, when you say it like that, Mabel, I sound like a real jerk."

Which is probably an accurate overall assessment of my character.

Ever since I ran out of the signing, I can't shake the feeling that what I said to Ralph was wrong.

He wasn't the jerk.

It was me.

"Wait," Mabel says. "Aren't you supposed to be on your bone-iversary trip with Ralph?"

"Yeah. I am, but—"

Louise clears her throat. "I object to the use of the word bone-iversary when my brother's bone is the bone in question."

"You really need to get over that, sister friend," I say. "I'm boning your brother for life. Deal with it." I flashback to the scene in the signing room. "At least I think I am."

"Whoa," Louise says. "Trouble in paradise?"

"Sort of. But look, I don't want my personal stuff to take time away from our Rich Bitch Power Hour."

Mabel raises her hand. "I'm still not sure about that group name for us."

"What?" I say. "We decided to reclaim the word bitch."

"Actually, *you* decided to reclaim the word bitch."

Right. Because Mabel has surely never been called a bitch in her life. Why would she? She's a damn angel.

Mabel continues, "My vote was for Science Sistas. Or STEM Fatales. Oh, I also really liked Entreprewhores."

About a year ago, Mabel, Louise, and I realized that the three of us had something unique in common. We're all scientists who started out on the usual path but then stumbled into becoming entrepreneurs. I went from museum life to writing. Mabel went from teaching bug classes at nature camps to running her own honey-making business. And Louise worked at an aquarium but now lives in Hawaii, where she co-runs a water excursion company and leads painting workshops on the beach.

So we decided to gather virtually once a week to chat about our challenges and celebrate our wins. It's been amazing to have this kind of support. They always have a way of helping me see things from a new perspective. Which is probably why I was so eager to take this call.

"I'm sure the right name will come to us eventually," Louise says. "But for now, let's hand the proverbial baton to Calliope. Clearly, she's the one in most need of the floor."

"Is it that obvious?" I say.

She nods. "You look like you're going to combust. Spill, woman. What the hell happened?"

"Your brother is a cocky bastard with an ego the size of a Titanosaur."

"You're talking about Ralph? The guy who loves sudoku and never misses the opportunity to crochet while listening to StarTalk radio on Sundays?"

"Yup, that's him. Today, his true colors came out, and they were garish as hell." I try to say this with confidence, but blaming Ralph for how everything went down doesn't feel right.

"Garish? Like parsley?" Mabel asks.

"No, that's a garnish," I say. "*Garish*. Obtrusively bright. Showy. Lurid."

"I don't like when you do that," Mabel says. "When you define a word with another word that needs to be defined."

I sigh. "Which one? Lurid?"

"Yeah, what's lurid?"

"Vividly shocking or sensational. Explicit. You know I get lexical when I'm upset."

Mabel's nose scrunches. "You're still doing it."

"Lexical means—"

Louise steps in, "No one cares. Just tell us what happened."

"Ralph embarrassed the hell out of me and created a scene at my signing."

"What did he do, whip out his penis or something?" Louise laughs.

I hesitate.

"Oh my God, he didn't whip out his penis, did he!?"

"No. But he came pretty damn close."

Louise's mouth drops open.

"Hey, have you ever noticed that people only use the word whip when it comes to penises?" Mabel says.

"That is inherently untrue," I respond. "Cream. Potatoes. Ass. You can whip many things."

"True. Sorry. Let me rephrase. Have you ever noticed that the penis is the only *body part* people say gets whipped out?" Mabel explains. "You've used that phrase in your books, Calliope, haven't you?"

"It's possible."

Mabel continues, "Yeah, I think in *The Velociraptor Factor*, Franz whipped it out a lot. But that makes sense for a dinosaur. Dinosaurs are super athletic. And don't get me wrong, my man Wally is in excellent shape, but I can honestly say I've never seen him *whip* out his penis. Present it, sure. Reveal it, display it? Absolutely. But whip it? Nah. Sounds fun, though. Whip! Whip! Whipwhipwhipwhip!"

Mabel embarks on a one-woman imaginary penis saber fight,

cracking herself up.

Louise says, "Let it be known that I'm only allowing this to continue because Iris and James headed out to the backyard."

"Oh good!" Mabel says. "Hope they have fun. Hey, I wonder if we can whip out our vaginas? Should one of us try?"

Mabel's parents kept her pretty sheltered as a kid. That led to her not having much of a friend group back then. So now that she's a grown woman free to do—and say—what she pleases, she tends to go a bit buck wild and sends us on some serious tangents. It's part of her charm.

"Mabel, if your vagina is whipping, you should probably see a doctor," I say.

"Totally. Okay, enough of that. You've gotten us off track, friend."

"*I've* gotten us off track?" I murmur.

"You have. Come on, give us the scoop!"

So I tell them all about our trip so far. About our less-than-ideal induction into the Mile High Club. How Ralph got recognized right away when we entered the hotel. How readers seemed way more interested in meeting him than me. And how he turned the signing event into an almost-strip show.

"Wow," Louise says. "That's not the brother I know. What do you think got into him?"

"No idea."

Mabel says, "Let me make sure I have this all clear. He's giving up his weekend to assist you, right?"

"Right," I say.

"And he did the impromptu performance after your idol asked him to, right?"

"Right."

"And people enjoyed it, right?"

"Right."

"So... what's the problem? Did it affect book sales?"

"Yeah, it did!"

"That sucks," Mabel continues. "No one bought any?"

"No, *everyone* bought them! I wouldn't be surprised when I go back if we're completely sold out!"

"Huh," Louise and Mabel say at the same time.

"What?"

I brace myself for the tough love I know is coming.

Louise and Mabel silently wrestle with who should level with me first. Unsurprisingly, Louise takes on the task. She's typically the voice of reason in this group.

"It sounds like maybe you're not as upset with Ralph as you are with yourself."

I scoff, but I already know she's right. "What does that mean?"

"You aren't a fan of emotions."

"What? I love emotions! My books are full of emotion."

"Yeah, your books are, but in real life, you avoid emotions like the plague."

I open my mouth to respond, but Louise holds up a finger to stop me.

"And before you get defensive and say you don't avoid happiness and excitement and all the other positive emotions—"

Damn, I was going to say that.

"Of course you don't. Everyone likes happiness and excitement. No one *likes* insecurity, jealousy, or shame, but they show up for all of us. Trying to avoid feeling them is a losing battle."

"Who are you, Brene Brown?"

She smiles. "I am your sister friend, and I want the best for you."

Oh crap, she's being Sincere Louise.

I'm way more comfortable with Sarcastic Louise.

She continues, "It sounds like your feelings were hurt today, which is totally understandable. But instead of lashing out at Ralph, who does sound like he went off the rails, and sabotaging the opportunity you created for yourself, maybe you could have acknowledged your feelings instead? And worked through those feelings with him?" She pauses. "He loves you. Even when he's an oblivious bonehead."

"Ugh. Why are you so good at this stuff?"

Louise gives a self-deprecating laugh. "Only for my friends. I'm crap at navigating my own shit."

"It's true!" Mabel says. "You saw what a mess Lou was when she and James were getting together. And I'm sensing a setback now that she's knocked up. Calliope, have you noticed whenever the baby subject comes up, she seems a little—"

"Nope!" Louise cuts her off. "This segment of our power hour isn't about me. It's all about Callie."

Suddenly, I feel an energy beside me.

I don't need to look up to know who it is.

Because when the person you love enters a room, you know it. You feel it.

"Guys, I actually have to cut this power hour short. The bonehead has arrived."

"Say no more, sister friend," Louise says.

"Heard you whipped it out in public, Ralphie!" Mabel shouts. "Good for you!"

"Okay, I'm signing off!" I shout back and close out the window on my phone.

I reach out and take his hand.

He gives it a squeeze.

"Head back to the room with me?" I ask.

"I'd love to." He smiles and pulls me to my feet, then his brow furrows. "I know things got a bit out of hand, but I didn't actually whip out my penis, did I?"

I laugh. "You came close, Ralph-alpha. You came real close."

Chapter Eight

CALLIOPE

We walk hand in hand through the casino in silence while slot machine bells ring all around us.

He's the only person I've ever been this comfortable with. Comfortable enough to be quiet. With most people, I feel a need to chat and to be witty and smart and fun. With Ralph, though, I can just be.

Trouble is, right now there is a world of words I want to get off my chest.

But I need to get him alone first.

We pass through the massive lobby and are almost to the elevators when a voice calls out, "Oh honey, there you are!"

It's Joella.

God, what she must think of me after I abandoned my table like that.

"You have a minute for that chat?" she asks.

My heart starts to pound. I point toward the elevator. "Hi, Joella. Thank you, but, um, that's okay. I'm sure you're super busy, and we were just going to—"

"Hey, Cosmo Kramer," she shouts to Ralph. "Tell your girlfriend I need to speak with her. It's imperative."

"It's, um, it's Rock Cosmos, actually," Ralph says with a smile. "And I'm not sure if you've noticed, Joella, but I don't *tell* Calliope—I mean, Tracy—anything."

"Ha, Good man. And geez! Why do I keep getting your pseudonym wrong?" She laughs and slaps Ralph on the back. "Cosmo Kramer is the guy on *Seinfeld*, right?"

"Right," he says.

"Well, regardless, I'm stealing your lady for a minute. Cool if she catches up with you in just a bit?"

Ralph squeezes my hand, then lets it go. "I'll meet you upstairs when you're done, okay?"

"You sure?" I ask.

"Absolutely," he says and heads into the elevator.

"You saved my butt today, sir!" Joella calls to him just as the silver doors start sliding closed.

He gives her a little salute, and then he's gone.

Joella wraps her arm around my shoulders and guides me to the cocktail lounge connected to the lobby. "You and I are having a drink, miss." She senses my hesitation. "Don't worry, I won't keep you long, but I have a few things to say to you."

Ordinarily, I'd give my left lung to spend quality time with Joella Flanders, but right now, I'd like nothing more than to avoid this. For a few reasons. One, I'm dying to get upstairs and make things right with Ralph. And two? I'm terrified she'll tell me I'm banned from her future book events because I acted like a damn chump.

We slide onto a pair of leather barstools, and Joella immediately signals the number two to the bartender.

"I'm treating you to my signature drink," she says.

Of course Joella has a signature drink. And of course the bartender knows her and loves her. I'm certain people bow down to serve her wherever she goes.

And rightly so.

The bartender places two frothy pink concoctions in front of us in record time.

"Cheers, Calliope." She lifts her glass.

"Cheers." I clink my glass with hers, but I can't keep the surprise out of my voice. "You, um. You called me Calliope."

"That's who I'm having a drink with, aren't I?" she asks. "You're Calliope right now. Not Tracy. You gotta learn to keep them separate." She takes a sip of her drink and continues, "Do not give away your self-worth to others. Ever."

"Okay..." I say, not a clue what she's getting at.

"You mentioned before that your career has been 'up and down and all around.' Believe me when I say, that's the nature of things, baby. But no matter what's happening out there..." Joella points toward the lobby, where readers roll their carts filled with signed paperbacks. "You have to stay steady here." She places a hand on her heart. "This is a tricky business, honey. We write because we love to tell stories. We hope readers will love those stories. Sometimes they do. But a lot of times, they don't." She shrugs, then leans closer and lowers her voice. "Sweetheart, one day they light your ass on fire with praise. The next day? They kick your beating heart into a dumpster, pour a bucket of lard on top of it, and set the whole fucking thing ablaze with gasoline."

The woman certainly has a way with words.

"I'm sorry if this sounds bitchy," I say. "But... how would you know? You're the most beloved writer out there."

She cackles. "Are you kidding me right now? Girl, an international book club meets monthly for the sole purpose of trashing my books. It's called Flanders Commanders. They dress up like military commanders, line my books up like a firing squad, then shoot them to smithereens."

"Oh my God, are you serious?"

She laughs. "No. I'm just kidding about that. But there is a group of women in Phoenix who rage read one of my books every month, then bond over everything they hated about it and post spoilers online."

I run my finger around the rim of my glass. "So they hate your books, but they read one every single month?"

"Go figure, right?" She chuckles some more. "I mostly laugh my way to the bank, but some nights I also cry myself to sleep." Her face softens, and she pats my hand. "We're human, Calliope. When people say shitty things about us, it hurts. But if you take it all too much to heart, you'll walk through your life hungry for compliments and always feel jealous when someone else is being fed."

Ralph's face flashes in my mind.

I remember how happy he was while performing in front of all those fans.

And how I couldn't find it in my heart to be happy for him.

I sigh and nod.

Joella knocks back the rest of her drink, then stands. She places a hand on my shoulder. "Don't believe your hype. Don't believe your haters. The truth lies somewhere in between. Find a way to bridge that gap, and the journey will be well worth taking, I promise." She pauses for dramatic effect. "Now, go get your man. Drinks are on me!" she tosses over her shoulder as she walks away.

I watch how people's faces light up as she makes her way through the lobby. They love her. She hugs another author, and they dive into a lively, heartfelt discussion. I'm astounded by her. She organizes this whole event, sells thousands of her own books like a boss, and still finds time to drop nuggets of wisdom and raise spirits wherever she's needed. She should change her title to *New York Times* Bestselling Author and Official Angsty Author Whisperer.

She's amazing.

The guy waiting for me in our room is pretty amazing too.

Time to face the music.

I leave a tip for the bartender and make my way upstairs. I knock on our door. I'm not sure why.

"It's me," I say.

"Why are you knocking? Get in here already." Ralph's voice echoes from inside.

I wave my card over the sensor and enter the room, where I find the place strangely quiet. And empty.

"Ralph?" I call.

"I'm in here," he says from the next room.

I take one step into the bathroom, and my mouth drops. Music softly plays. Steam fogs up the mirrors. Little bowls of candy and treats surround the clawfoot porcelain tub. And inside the tub is the most beautiful man I know, naked as the day he was born, submerged in bubbles.

"You have your Clark Kent hair happening," I say with a happy sigh.

He shrugs and disturbs a few bubbles. "I know you like it."

He pats his hands along his usually shaggy hair, which is wet and combed into a side part.

"I do. It's deliciously geeky."

"Get in with me," he says. "I know you do your best brainstorming in the tub."

I unbutton my shirt and shimmy down my skirt. His eyes take in every movement I make until I've completely undressed. I strike a pose that makes him laugh.

"So whaddaya got? You have a new series idea?" I ask as I dip my toes into the steamy water, then fully immerse myself.

"Not exactly," he says.

One of our favorite things to do at home is sink into our bathtub and toss around wild story ideas for my future books. But our bathtub at home certainly doesn't look—or feel—like this.

This feels like heaven.

But I think that has way more to do with the man whose arms and legs wrap around me than the tub's size or the water's temperature. I'm so relieved to be back in his arms after a dumb day.

"So what are we brainstorming?" I give him my full weight and lean back into his chest.

"We're brainstorming us," he says. "How do we want *our* story to go?"

I jerk my head around to look at him and accidentally splash him in the eye.

"Is this your opener for breaking up with me?"

"Breaking up with you?" He grabs a fluffy white towel and dabs at his face. "Do you really think I'd get you naked and all loved up in the tub with me just to break up with you? On our bone-iversary weekend, no less?"

"It does seem like a weird way to end things," I admit. "Unless you wanted to get in one last screw. Because people can say what they want about me, but we all know I can screw."

He laughs. "Yes. We all know you can screw." He kisses me slow and deep. "Calliope?"

"Yeah?" I say, a bit breathless.

"I'm never breaking up with you."

"Never?" I whisper.

He shakes his head. "This is it for me. *You're* it for me."

"Oh, thank God." I kiss him, then let out a flood of words. "I was a jerk today, Ralph-alpha. You were right on the plane. I was nervous as hell about this whole thing. I read one too many nasty reviews recently, and my confidence took a friggin' nosedive. So when I saw you getting all that attention today and being so free and happy with everyone, I guess I lashed out. If I hadn't been hiding from my reviews like a scared little punk, I might have been more supportive and prepared for Rock Cosmos, Audio Sensation. I'm sorry. Also are those dino gummies?"

I point at one of the small candy bowls around the tub.

"They are," he says and feeds me one.

God, I love him.

"Wait. Let's backtrack a second. My girl? Scared?" He wraps his arms around me tighter. "Never."

"All the time, actually," I fight the tears that want to well in my eyes.

He nuzzles my neck and nibbles on my ear. "Well then, you should talk to me about that stuff from now on. That's why I'm here."

"*That's* why you're here?" I lean into him as he continues to kiss down my neck.

"Well, that.... and the other stuff." His voice goes all Rock Cosmos on me, and I can't be mad at today's readers for a single second. That voice is my kryptonite too.

His hands go under water, and "the other stuff" he alluded to begins. But just as things heat up, he stops us.

"Hold on, hold on," he whispers. "Before things get out of hand, because, knowing you, they will get out of hand—"

"But you like out of hand," I say and try to continue moving things in the direction he started.

"I do, but seriously, just a second, Callie." He takes both my hands in his, then clears his throat. "You're not the only one who could have done things differently today. I was an egotistical maniac." He sounds surprised.

"You were, weren't you?" I laugh.

"It was the craziest thing. When I walked in that room, I was a semi-humble guy there to support my girlfriend. But then, all it took was a few people saying my voice was sexy, and I morphed into a pelvis-pumping lunatic."

"You did put on quite a show," I say. "But I shouldn't have left you there."

"Yeah, you should have." He sighs. "What I said to you was..." He hesitates. "Well, it was a low blow. The whole 'No one can make you feel a certain way' bullshit? And 'if you feel unseen or unappreciated, that's on you'? I'm sure I butchered the message, but I heard something like that on this therapy podcast thing Lou likes, and instead of actually taking it to heart, I used it to be a dick to you. Because *I* was the one feeling... ugh, this is what makes me a cinnamon roll, right? All this emotional oozing I'm doing?"

I laugh. "Sort of, yeah. But it's good. A lot of guys aren't great at this stuff. Hell, *I'm* not great at this stuff. What did you call it? Emotional Intelligence 101?"

He cringes. "Again, I was a dick." He leans his head back on the rim of the tub. "I think I had this story in my head that you were disappointed in me. In the way my life has been going lately."

"Oh my God, that's ridiculous."

"Think about it, though. Your hot astronomer turned into a kiddie party planner. Not exactly what you signed up for."

"So you think you're hot, huh?" I smile and snuggle closer to him.

"Please don't make this hard," he says.

"You don't want me to make you hard?" I run my hands through his tiny bit of chest hair. "Now, *that* is disappointing."

"Just let me finish."

"I always let you finish."

"Callie?" he says in his serious voice.

"Sorry."

"When you grow up with a dream as big as becoming an astronaut and don't come remotely close to accomplishing it, it's easy to walk around feeling like you missed the mark. And look, I know that probably ninety percent of little kids say they want to be an astronaut at some point, but I *really* wanted it for a long time. I was the twelve-year-old kid checking aeronautical engineering books out of the library and googling what college majors would most likely get me into space. That was the plan. The only plan." He exhales heavily. "So when that fell away, and planetarium work was no longer in the cards either, I panicked. Ya know, a quiet panic so you couldn't see. And I acted like the party planning stuff was actually where I wanted to be."

"But it wasn't," I say.

"Hell no." He pauses, and his voice softens. "But narrating for you? I kind of love it. And the feedback from listeners this weekend? Well, it didn't suck. It felt like something was finally moving in the right direction. Also, part of me probably thought if you saw all those women going crazy over me, you'd be proud to be with me. So I went overboard."

I scoot the bowl of dino gummies closer to us and feed him a piece.

"For the record, I'm always proud to be with you. Now and forever." I grab a washcloth and lather it up with soap. "And that's true whether you're leading birthday parties, or working in planetariums, or spewing filth into microphones all over the world." I run the washcloth down his neck and over his chest. "In the future, though, if you feel compelled to go all Magic Mike at one of my book events, a heads-up would be nice."

"I can do that." He closes his eyes and luxuriates while I wash him. "In my defense, we did sell a ton of books."

"We did?"

"Oh yeah. Our table got totally cleared out, and I started a list three pages long for folks who prepaid and want us to ship to them."

"That's incredible!" I pause. "*Us*, though? You want to keep helping with that sort of thing?"

He opens his eyes, and I still my hand over his heart. "That is what I'm saying. I want to do more than help, Calliope. I want to be really in this with you. I realize my first foray into assisting you might not have been my best foot forward, but yes, I want to be your partner. In everything."

My eyes well with tears. Happy ones this time.

"You can't keep doing everything on your own, right?" he says. "Not if you want to keep growing."

"That's true. I actually have been thinking recently about finding a PA."

"Does that stand for piece of ass?" He smirks.

I laugh. "Usually, it stands for personal assistant. But if you want the job, we can definitely make 'piece of ass' your honorary title for now and see where things go."

"I accept the position." He flips us around so he's hovering above me, water splashing and sloshing out of the tub. "And I'm confident you'll like where things are about to go."

I give myself over to the bliss of being with this man and let out a sigh of pleasure. "Looks like someone is well on his way to a promotion."

Epilogue

RALPH

"Are we hiking in the dark? Is that what your surprise is? Hiking in the dark after midnight and getting murdered by coyotes?"

I hold her hand as we trudge toward the spot all the websites say is the best. Our hair is still wet from our bathtub shenanigans, but the desert air will take care of that in no time.

"We are not going to get murdered by coyotes, Callie. I have done my due diligence, and I promise you I am taking you somewhere safe and beautiful."

"Okay," she says, doubt still in her voice. "Because I don't know if you've noticed, but it's dark AF out here."

"True. Darkness is sort of a prerequisite for what I have in mind." I turn us onto the walking trail that I scoped out online. "It should be about a hundred feet this way."

"So you and Joella are book besties now, huh?" Calliope says as we walk. "You were strangers just this morning, and now she lets you drive her rental car into the middle of the desert like it's no big deal?"

"You're really hard to surprise, do you know that?" I laugh, but it's clear she's waiting for an explanation. "I told Joella today at the signing that I was planning a grand romantic gesture of sorts, and she readily offered her support."

"That sounds like Joella. But really, what romance author doesn't like a grand romantic gesture? We live for this shit." She pauses. "Just checking, though. You're not going to propose to me, right? Because we've both decided that—"

"Callie? You have to stop living in fear that I'm going to propose to you. It's you and me forever. But no, I don't need that piece of paper either. I'm happy for other people when they go that route, but that's just not us."

"And that's okay, right?"

"It's more than okay. This is our life. We make the rules."

I give her a quick kiss.

"I love when you unintentionally quote Taylor Swift songs," she says. "Okay, good. Glad we're still on the same page about that because I really want us to be that sexy old couple who dies together at a hundred years old as boyfriend and girlfriend. That's hot, isn't it?"

"Mmm. Old people. Death. So hot," I joke.

She gives me a playful shove. "Shut up. You know what I mean."

We arrive at a fenced-in area, and I open the gate. "Here we are." I take in her confused expression and nod toward the fence. "To keep the coyotes out."

Calliope takes tentative steps inside the enclosure where I immediately unfurl the blanket I've been carrying, spread it on the ground, and take a seat.

"Join me, will you?" I reach out for her hand.

She looks skeptical as she takes my hand and sits beside me. "What are we doing?"

"Shhh. Lie back with me."

In an out-of-character moment for Calliope, she follows my request with no quips and no argument.

"Now, look up," I say.

And she does.

The most gorgeous, expansive, star-filled sky I've ever seen stretches out above us.

"Holy shit!" she shouts, then lowers her voice to a near whisper. "Excuse my language, but that is fucking phenomenal. I've never seen a sky that looks like this. There have to be like a zillion stars up there."

"Astronomers estimate there are approximately two hundred billion."

"Two hundred billion stars?" She stares up in awe.

"Yeah, and that's just in our galaxy. You have to figure millions upon millions of other galaxies have their own potential two hundred billion stars. Though the Milky Way is a medium-sized galaxy. Plenty of galaxies are far bigger. The biggest galaxy we know of is called IC 1101, which has over one hundred *trillion* stars. We'll likely never know the exact number of stars in the Universe at large, but—"

"Got it, baby." She squeezes my hand. "There are a fuck ton of stars in that sky."

I laugh. "A fuck ton. Yes."

We continue to stare at the sky and contemplate it all.

"Thanks for bringing me here," she whispers. "This is the perfect way to feel grounded again after an insane day."

"Thank you for being here with me," I whisper back. "Can you believe that out of all the planets in all the galaxies in all of the Universe, we ended up here? Together?"

She turns her pretty head to look at me. "Meant to be, I guess."

I kiss her softly on the lips. "Meant to be."

"I was thinking, when we're a hundred and hot and dying together..."

"Oh, are we back to that?"

"We are. We're back to that." She props herself up on an elbow. "Maybe the boyfriend/girlfriend title isn't sufficient after a lifetime of loving each other, you know? At that point, we might want and deserve a title with more substance."

"Alright. What are you thinking?"

"I don't know. Manfriend and womanfriend sounds kind of dumb. Lover is a little better, but if I'm being honest, when people call each other lover, it gives me the creeps."

"What if we're just Ralph and Callie?" I reach out a hand and stroke her cheek.

She smiles and kisses my palm. "I like that."

Calliope lowers back to the blanket and curls into me, her head resting in the crook between my chest and shoulder.

"Yeah." I pull her closer as a shooting star arcs overhead. "Ralph and Callie sounds perfect."

Buggin'

Chapter One

MABEL

"Welcome to another episode of 'Honey, I'm Home! With Your Favorite Redhead, Mabel McGonigle' where we talk about making honey and making love! But not in that order. That would be sticky. And not the good kind of sticky! Hahaha!" I pause and reconsider what I just said. "But I guess making love and *then* making honey wouldn't exactly be sanitary either. Anyhoo, I'm your host Mabel McGonigle, and today, my sidekick, Walla-Walla Bing Bang, and I are teaching you how to harvest!"

I exhale and lock eyes with the beautiful, burly man behind the camera.

"Was that too much?" I unzip my bee suit and fan myself with the flaps.

Wally stops recording. "Mabey Baby, you're always the right amount of much."

"Awwww." Even after two years together, this man can still make me blush. "I just didn't know if directly comparing honey to sexual fluids might be taking things a step too far. But it's never a bad thing to encourage cleanliness in the workplace, right?"

"Right," he says. "And what's taking things too far? The numbers don't lie. People love you exactly as you are. Unfiltered and adorable."

"Oh I wanna smoosh you."

"Smoosh away, baby."

I run and straddle jump him.

He catches me with ease and kisses me deep.

"Are we really sticking with Walla-Walla Bing Bang as my

sidekick nickname, though?" he says when we come up for air.

"We are." I nod.

"What my lady wants, my lady gets." Wally sighs good-naturedly and gives me another kiss before placing me back on my feet. "One quick idea for a retake, though?"

"Of course!" I run back into position next to one of my beehives.

"We might want to specify *what* we're harvesting. If we just dangle the whole 'today we're going to teach you how to harvest' thing, people might assume we're harvesting bodies for organs."

"Ooooooh." I shudder. "You really think they'd assume that?"

He shrugs. "Hard to say. This is only our eighth episode, and so far, we've swung pretty broadly between beekeeping, redhead trivia, and tips for keeping a nudist home. We're still a bit of a wildcard. Plus, this is the first time they're seeing you in your full beekeeping gear. At first glance, it could double as a kill suit."

"Ooooooh." I shudder again. "Thank you for that feedback. Okay, I'll get more specific on this next take."

Wally sets the camera up for the shot while I rezip my suit and shake out my limbs.

"I'm not spreading us too thin, am I? All the advice I've been getting from other Youtubers is to 'niche it down,' but I dunno, should I really 'niche it down' on my passions? I tried, but I just can't pick! Bugs, buns, and redhead puns. I love 'em all!"

"Don't change a damn thing, you." He winks.

This guy has my heart.

I attempt a wink back, but I end up giving him an open-mouthed, two-eyed blink.

I've always admired people who can make winking look effortlessly sexy.

That person is not me.

He laughs. "Alright. In three, two..."

Wally counts us down on his fingers and presses record.

I launch back in. "Welcome to another episode of 'Honey, I'm Home! With Your Favorite Redhead, Mabel McGonigle' where we talk about..."

Wally's feedback was spot-on, and the next take is perfect.

Sometimes I can't believe this is my life.

I live on a tree farm with this amazing man, who literally built our dream home with his own two hands. I teach kids all things entomology at the museum and the arboretum a few mornings a week, then I come back to our little haven where twelve hives and over five hundred thousand bees wait for me to make gooey, golden magic with them. The Bee's Elbow, my one-woman honey operation, is doing well for an up-and-coming local business. I sell honey-infused soaps, candles, body butter, you name it. But my biggest seller by far is my raw, edible honeycombs.

Last month during one of our entreprewhore sessions—that's what I'm calling our support group whether the other two like it or not—Calliope suggested I could give The Bee's Elbow a business boost by launching a YouTube channel. She said I'm a "character" and "inherently watchable"—whatever that means—and that a show I hosted would be a guaranteed hit. So Wally and I made it happen. And what do you know? It's working! We have over forty thousand subscribers and counting. My online orders for The Bee's Elbow are steadily climbing, and it seems like exciting new opportunities are popping up for us every single day.

"Oh my gosh, Walla-Walla, the coolest thing happened today!" I take a swig from my water bottle and hand his to him as well. He takes a sip. "Whew! It's hot as a scrotum today, isn't it?"

He spits the water right out of his mouth. "A scrotum?"

"Shoot! Is it testicles? You know I don't always get sayings right." "Balls, Mabes." He laughs. "The saying is hot as balls."

"Right, right. Gotcha. It's hot as *balls* today, honeybun. Make sure you stay hydrated."

He tips his bottle up to me and smiles. "I shall. So what's the good news?" He chugs his water.

"Hm?" It's easy to get lost in his beautiful smile. In the way his throat moves while he drinks. In everything about him, really.

Most days, I can't believe he's mine.

Wally takes my hand and guides me to a wooden two-seater swing we have hanging between a pair of sturdy trees. He sits and pats the space beside him. I sit and drape my legs across his lap.

"You said the coolest thing happened today," he reminds me.

"Right. Yes. Okay, brace yourself."

"Consider me braced."

"Want to go to the Netherlands with me?" I squeal.

"Wow." His eyebrows scrunch together. "Well, yeah. Of course! I want to go everywhere with you. What's in the Netherlands?"

I clap my hands. "Redheads. So many redheads!"

"You're the only redhead I need, lady." He caresses my cheek. "But tell me more."

"Declan messaged me this morning and told me all about this National Redhead Day Festival that happens in the Netherlands where he lives. He goes every year and says it's awesome. He thinks I should go."

"Declan thinks you should go?" His eyes get wide and weird.

"Well, he thinks *we* should go."

"Does he now?"

I sigh. "Your voice is doing that thing again."

"What thing?"

"The thing where you sound all angry and jealous, but you're trying to be supportive and sweet. How many times do I have to tell you that he is just one of our followers who likes what we do?"

He scoffs. "He likes what *you* do, that's clear."

I grab his scruffy chin and turn his head to face me. "Hold on a second. Don't we want people to like what I do?"

"Sure, we do. But we don't need them all sliding into your DMs and inviting you overseas to their motherland."

"It's not his motherland, actually. Declan is from California. He went to the Redhead Festival a few years ago with his family, and they loved it so much, they decided to stay."

He cocks his head to the side. "How well do you know this guy?"

"I don't know." I shrug. "We chat!"

"How often?"

"Just like three or four times."

His face relaxes a bit. "Alright."

"A day," I add.

"You chat with this man three or four times a *day?*" Wally says so loudly a flock of birds scatters from the tree above us.

"Yeah." I shrug my shoulders again. "He's really nice. Anyway,

I haven't even told you the best part yet! I did some research on the festival and ended up reaching out to the woman in charge of booking vendors. The event is in less than a month, so of course the deadline to apply is way past, but listen to this! She just had someone cancel yesterday, so she has an opening! She checked out a few of our episodes and told me if The Bee's Elbow wants the spot, it's ours! Isn't that incredible? I mean, how great will this be? I've never been to Europe, and I reeeeeeally want to. So we can travel—which you know I've always wanted to do—bond with redheads—which you know I've always wanted to do, *and* we can make new business connections and customers at the same time! Are you in? Oh, please tell me you're in."

He sighs, then smiles that glorious smile I love so much.

"Mabel? If you're in, I'm in. Always."

Chapter Two

WALLY

*I*f you told me two years ago that I'd be wearing all white and marching the cobblestone streets of Europe with a sea of over eight thousand gingers, I'd call you a damn liar.

To be fair, though, I didn't see a lot of things in my future two years ago.

People, for one thing.

Back then, I couldn't care less if I interacted with a single person for weeks on end. I was content working the land at Bucks County Arboretum, living in my little one-person tiny home, and avoiding humans as much as possible—with the occasional exception made for a beer with my buddy James.

But then Mabel entered my world and turned everything upside down.

Who the hell have I become?

I'm marching in a redhead parade.

Wearing white linen drawstring pants.

With a leather satchel slung over my shoulder.

And I'm head over ass in love with the adorable woman skipping by my side.

"Ohmygarshk, I love twinning with you!" Mabel twirls beside me in a flowy white sundress. She smacks me square on the ass and tugs my waistband. "You sure you're okay with these drawstring jobbies? I know they're not your usual style, but I couldn't find Carhartt utility work pants in white. And I tried. Hard."

"They're great." I kiss her on the forehead. "Very... breezy."

The couple parading directly in front of us looks back at us and smiles. Actually, they don't look at *us*. They look at *me*. A full up-and-down perusal of my entire body.

I lean closer to Mabel's ear and whisper, "That's not the first time they've done that. What's going on? Is it because I'm not a redhead?"

"No way! The parade FAQ emphatically stated, 'We welcome everyone, including the blonde, the brunette, and the bald.'"

"What about folks with white, gray, or silver hair?"

"Yup! There's a clause about them too! As long as you wear white and support redheadedness, you are welcome to march. Hey, did you know that redheads aren't likely to ever go gray? Most of us will just lose pigment over time and appear blond. Perhaps white. But almost never gray."

So many redhead facts are coming my way during this trip.

Let's see if I can impress her with this one.

"Did *you* know that even though redheads only make up two percent of the world's population, over thirty percent of primetime commercials include a person with red hair?"

"Because we're hot!" she says.

"You'll get no arguments from me on that one." I wrap my arm around her as we continue to march.

"But no, I did not know that!" she says. "How do *you* know that?"

"You know me, I keep my eyes and ears open, baby. Also, I picked up a 'Fifteen Fun Facts About Red Hair' pamphlet at the welcome desk when you were checking us in."

The couple in front of us sneaks a peek at me again.

"Alright, what gives?" I ask Mabel, but I purposely keep my voice loud enough that the creepers in front of us can hear.

A cute little cringe crosses Mabel's face. "I have to tell you something."

"What is it?" I ask.

"I only just noticed it myself. And believe me, I'm not complaining. I mean, who would complain? Look at you. You're *so*—"

"Spit it out, Mabes."

"Okay. Come here."

She takes both my hands in hers and pulls us to the side, out of step with the rest of the redheads. She guides us into an alleyway speckled with flowerpots and presses me up against the stone wall.

"Alright, I see where you're going with this," I rumble as I pull Mabel closer and skate my lips down her neck.

"Oooooh." She shudders. "That's my spot. You know that's my spot."

"Of course, I know that's your spot. I know all your spots."

"Your pants are see-through!" she shouts.

This freezes me right in place, mid-kiss on her collarbone.

"Excuse me?" I rise to my full height.

"I'm sorry!" She winces, then completely changes expressions. "But I'm also sorry *not* sorry. Is that the expression? Because..." She looks directly at my crotch. "Mm-mm-mm and yumma-lumma-ding-dong."

Even when I'm annoyed with her, she can always make me laugh.

I look down and pull at the fabric. "Mabey Baby," I say calmly. "You told me they *weren't* see-through."

"They weren't! Not when you asked me back at the flat, that is. But once we hit the sun?" She sighs. "Yeah, then everyone could see everything."

"Are you telling me I just paraded through a foreign city while publicly dangling my dong?"

"Yes, but who cares! You did us all a favor! Shine your light, bright angel! You know I'm all about the nudity!"

"At home, yeah." I laugh nervously. "But this is... different."

Mabel had a unique reaction two years ago when she learned her family had lied to her about her real parents. Many people would go to therapy. And she did do a bit of that. But what helped her most was learning to let her personal freak flag fly. She'd spent so much of her life up to that point being a good girl and following other people's orders, and all it left her with was a cheating ex-boyfriend and parents who deceived her. So now? She operates on instinct. And one of those instincts just happens to be... nudity. Whenever and wherever possible.

This is a beautiful thing that I fully support. But damn, we gotta choose our moments, don't we?

And this moment ain't it.

"You look amazing. I just thought you should know why you were getting such appreciative looks from people."

She makes another valiant attempt at a wink and tries pulling me back toward the parade.

I stop her. "Mabel, no. I need to go to the flat and put on some boxers."

"But you hate underwear!"

"True. But I hate arrests for indecent exposure even more."

"The only thing you'll be arrested for is being dead sexy," she purrs. "But, look, on the very off chance that an officer of the law notices your dinglehopper and creates a problem—"

"Please don't call it my dinglehopper," I interrupt, but she just keeps on going.

"Just use the 'does the rug match the lampshade' defense! Guys ask redheads that question all the time." She smiles and tosses her hair to the side.

After two amazing years with this woman, I still sometimes need clarification on how her brain works. It's a good thing, though. The best thing. She's the gift I get to keep opening and opening.

I clear my throat and try hard to hide the smile that wants to spread across my face. "What is the 'does the rug match the lampshade defense?'"

"Your *lampshade* may be sandy-colored." She tugs on my hair. "But your *rug*"—she cups my linen-covered balls—"is a redhead."

She presses me up against the wall again. I'm a weak, weak man when it comes to her, so I give in to her adorableness. We make out in the alleyway until—I can't help it—I have to set the record straight. On a few things.

"Mabey Baby?" I smooth her hair back and cup her cheeks with both hands.

"Hm?" She tilts her face up to me, eyes still closed in contentment.

I whisper, "The saying is actually 'Does the *carpet*"—I place her hand back on my crotch—"match the *drapes*?'" I let my shoulder-length hair hang down and tickle her cheek.

She smiles, then opens her eyes wide. "Really? Drapes? For hair head?"

"Yeah."

"But that doesn't make any sense! You are the sexy lamp." She runs her hands up and down the length of my body. "And your hair"—she gathers my strands into a ponytail and gives it a tug—"is the pretty shade on top. What are those dummies trying to say? That you're a big square window, and your hair is heavy, dreary *drapes*?" She scoffs. "No. Lampshade works way better."

"Alright, I'll give you that one. But Mabes, my rug? It may be *tinted*, but it's not a redhead."

"Like Conan," she says.

"The Barbarian?"

She shakes her head seriously. "O'Brien."

I open my mouth to protest, but she places a finger over my lips.

"Shhh. I spend way more time down there than you do. This is a good thing, Wally. Face it. You're a fire-crotch, and I'm the biotch fanning your flames."

Just then, the tail end of the parade goes past the alleyway entrance.

"Quick! We can still catch up with everyone!" she says.

"You go, Mabey Baby. I'm seriously not comfortable with my current state of affairs." I look down at my pants, which feel like they're getting thinner by the second. "You go finish the parade with the rest of the redheads, and I'll meet you at our table before it's go-time."

"You sure?" Her focus darts back and forth between me and the disappearing parade.

"Absolutely. I owe James a phone call anyway, so this will be a good opportunity to catch up." I give her a quick kiss. "I love you."

"Love you too, bugaboo! See you in a few!" she calls as she hustles away from me.

Don't ask her.

Don't ask her.

Dammit, I have to ask her.

"Hey!" I call just as she's about to exit the alleyway. "That Declan guy. He didn't ask you if your carpet matches your drapes, did he?"

"What?" Her face twists up in confusion.

"Never mind. I'm just—Forget I said anything."

"Hey, that reminds me! Declan said he'll swing by our booth this afternoon so we can finally meet IRL! That means 'in real life.' Eeeeeee!" she squeals.

"Eeeeee!" I half-heartedly squeal back. "Can't wait."

She blows me a kiss.

Then she's gone.

I lean against the brick wall and contemplate my next move.

After lengthening the strap length on my satchel and strategically placing the pouch over my... dear God, did my girlfriend tell me I have a fire-crotch? I walk out of the alley and walk in the opposite direction the parade went.

I pull out my phone and dial James. No doubt he would rag on me for using a "man purse" like this, but right now, I'm grateful to have it. Not only is it helping me reclaim my modesty, but it is carrying some seriously precious cargo. I reach my hand in there for what has to be the hundredth time today to check that the small square box is still there.

James picks up on the first ring and sounds out of breath when he says, "Did ya pop the question yet? What did she say?"

"Why are you breathing so heavy?" I ask. "You didn't pick up the phone mid-*session* did you?"

"Mid-session? What kind of session? What are you talking about?" James continues to huff and puff.

"I mean, I'm not interrupting you and Louise, am I?"

"Mind out of the gutter, pervert. I'm on a run. I'm running."

"Well, could you stop?" I laugh. "I feel like I'm listening to a porno starring my best friend. It's weird. And distracting."

"Gimme a second," he says. "I need some water."

I sit on a bench beside a fountain and listen to James chug on the other end of the phone.

"Ahh!" He makes that unnecessary sound some people make after drinking. "Look, Wallace. If it weren't for me throwing you and Mabel that impromptu beer date at the Artisan Festival two years ago, you wouldn't even have a lady to propose to right now, so will you just gimme the scoop without making me beg?"

"First of all, you're giving yourself way too much credit for helping Mabel and me get together. Second –"

"Did you or did you not end up in an outdoor shower with the woman less than an hour after I got all matchmakery on you?" He interrupts.

"We did, yeah, but I'll have you know that I was well on my way to making a move before you meddled."

James scoffs. "Sure. If by 'making a move,' you mean snarling and grumping your way through a life of loneliness and abstinence, then yeah. Sure, you were. You were really on a roll, fella."

"Geez, what crawled up your ass this morning? Louise still cranky?"

"I'm just –" He sighs. "Look, I don't begrudge the woman a little crank. She's seven months pregnant after all, but she's..." He trails off like he's not actually going to finish his sentence.

"She's what?" I prompt.

"She's been kinda mean lately!" he says. "I was hoping you called with a sweet proposal story to restore my faith in romance. But instead, you're holding out on me and giving me shit. So? Have you done it yet?"

"I have not."

"Come on, man!" he yells.

"Chill, will you?" I say. "I've been carrying the ring around with me nonstop, but I haven't found the right time to do it. Since we got here yesterday, it's been a whirlwind of unpacking, unintentionally showing all of Tilburg that *I'm* packing, parading with redheads, getting her vendor situation figured out—"

"Excuse me, what?" James chokes on the water he's chugging again. "Back up, back up, back up."

"To which part?"

"The part between unpacking and parading?"

"Oh. Yeah." I scrub my hands over my face, then double-check the positioning of my satchel. "Mabel got me new pants which— unbeknownst to me—put my cock on full display all morning. Whatever. It's not a big deal."

James snorts. "And you felt it necessary to tell me that you're *packing*? Feeling braggadocious today, are we, Wallace?"

"What? You want me to be disingenuous and pretend I'm not?" I laugh and wonder how the hell I got myself into this inane discussion.

"Good point. You could pretend, but I'd know you were lying. You forget, we grew up in locker rooms together."

"I do not forget," I say. "It's hard to forget the guy who walked around the locker room with a towel draped over his shoulder. And *only* his shoulder."

"So you got the goods on me too." I can hear the shrug in James's voice. "You know what? I'm glad this came up. I feel closer to you, man. How have we not talked about this before?"

"Because this is not a conversation most hetero male friends have?" I suggest.

"Well, we're not most hetero male friends, are we?"

"Fair enough," I say and check the time on my phone. "But listen, I only have a few minutes, and I did not call you to wax poetic about the size of my cock."

"So why did you call me then?" He pauses. "Oh snap! Are you asking me to be your best man, man?"

James's mood certainly has turned around during this phone call. After some friendly banter and a welcome opportunity to rag on me, he's back to his cheery light-hearted self.

"I... *wasn't*..." I start.

"Oh." James deflates.

"But of course you're gonna be my best man, man! Who else would it be?"

"Score!" he shouts.

"I just think I should make sure a wedding is even in the cards first before I start assembling a wedding party, you know?"

"Sure. That's smart." He pauses. "It's not like you to hesitate on something like this though. So? What's the real holdup?"

I take a deep breath and tell him the truth.

"I'm feeling like an overprotective, possessive asshole who doesn't deserve her."

"What? You? No way!"

Ordinarily, James would be right. I'm not that guy. The guy who sees the woman in his life as "his." The guy who needs to know where she is and who she's talking to at all times, or else he loses his damn mind. Mabel has had enough people in her life who underestimate her and try to control her. She won't get any of that bullshit from me.

But I just can't shake the feeling that something is up with this Declan dude.

And it's making me crazy.

I give James the whole backstory on the guy.

"What do you think? Am I overreacting?" I ask.

"Alright," James says. "You're telling me this D-Clan joker—"

"His name is Declan," I interrupt.

"Oh, I heard you the first time." James is getting fired up, I can tell. "I'm intentionally calling him D-Clan. You're telling me this D-Clan joker watches Mabel's YouTube show religiously, leaves constant comments about how sweet and pretty she is, slides into her DMs *multiple times a day*, and is the main catalyst for this trip overseas? And despite knowing that you are her co-producer on the YouTube show and her partner in life, he has never reached out to you personally?"

"That's what I'm telling you."

"Yeah, no. That guy's up to no good," he says definitively.

Shit. That's what I thought.

Chapter Three

MABEL

"*I*s that the prettiest girl on YouTube?" a male voice says the moment I reach my festival booth and raise our The Bee's Elbow flag.

I turn to see a redheaded man standing in front of me with a sweet, toothy grin.

"Declan? Oh my gosh, hi!"

He opens his arms. "Should we hug?"

"Absolutely! I love hugs!"

He picks me up and spins me around and around.

"This is bananas, isn't it?" he says into my hair as he continues to hold me tight. "Finally seeing each other in real life?"

"Beyond bananas, yeah!" I say.

He places me back on the ground, and we stand smiling at each other like goofballs.

What's truly bananas is how close I feel to this guy in such a short time. It's rare for me to have a friend who is a guy, let alone to feel so in sync with one I barely know.

I realize that I'm smiling so big my cheeks hurt.

This is okay, right?

I take stock of what's been happening between Declan and me these past few months. There's not an ounce of man-woman weirdness between us, I swear. Nothing inappropriate at all. He's just a new, platonic redhaired buddy. Kind of like the sweet cardinal who perches on my mailbox most mornings and makes me smile. Declan just perches in my YouTube comments and brightens my day by saying nice things.

And obviously my heart is set on Wally always and forever.

Wally did seem a little uncomfortable with this situation, though.

I shake off that thought. I'm sure as soon as he meets Declan, he'll see that there's nothing at all to worry about.

Declan squints toward my booth. "Where is the famous Wally? I thought he'd be here."

"He will! He, um. He had a small wardrobe malfunction and had to head back to the hotel and change. He should be here any minute."

"Great! I'm excited to meet him. Oh, before I forget..."

He wheels a cart I didn't see beside him closer to the booth. It's then I notice the word Volunteer emblazoned on his green shirt.

"I am going from booth to booth offering all the vendors our official Redhead Festival Survival Kit." He pulls a small canvas tote from the cart and hands it to me.

"Ooooh. Thank you." I quickly peer inside. "I didn't realize you were volunteering. I thought your band was playing this week."

"Double duty, baby! I'm volunteering during the day and playing with the band at night!" He rummages for something in his cart while he speaks. "We're actually playing tonight at this great little bar called *Bar*. You'll love it."

"The bar is called *Bar*?"

"Yup!" he says. "You know how it is today. All the cool places have these simple, obvious names. Like a salad place called *Fork*. An ice cream shop named *Spoon*. A bar called *Bar*. That's how you know it's a great spot. Here it is!"

He presents me with a postcard.

"'The Flamehead Family Singers.'" I read aloud, my head cocked to the side.

"Alright." He chuckles. "You got me. It's less of a *band* and more of an improvisational family singing group."

"You sing with your family?"

"Improvisationally, yes."

"Like you make up the songs on the spot?"

"Yes."

"Well, this I have to see!"

"So you'll come?" he says excitedly.

"I'll need to check with Wally first, but yes, I'd love to!"

"Amazing!"

We hug again. This time when we step apart, a weird moment of silence overtakes us both. It's not unpleasant at all, just... unexpected.

When our stare down verges on awkward, Declan says, "Your freckles. They don't really come across on camera. But in person?" He reaches out and gently pinches my cheek. "Wow."

"Hahaha. Thanks, I guess?"

"Definitely a compliment, yes." Declan continues to stare at me, then says, "You're a freckle lover, aren't you? Gosh, how have I never asked you this? Please tell me you're a freckle lover, or this friendship can't continue!"

"Of course I'm a freckle lover!" I give him a playful shove.

"Oh thank God." He places a dramatic palm over his heart. "It kills me how many people malign those mini pricks of melanin. Did you know that over eighty percent of redheads carry the freckle gene? For more redheaded trivia, be sure to check out the *Flamehaired Fun Facts*, one of several informational packets you'll find in your survival kit."

Why does Declan suddenly sound like he's giving a rehearsed speech?

"Are you okay, Declan?"

"I'm great, yeah! Why do you ask?"

"Well, you're breathing kind of fast, you're real sweaty all of a sudden, and calling freckles little pricks doesn't really seem like your style."

"My apologies to freckles everywhere," he says, avoiding eye contact. "As to why I am suddenly so sweaty? Well, this fucking sun, am I right?" He shields his eyes from the brightness. "That reminds me, Mabel. Sunscreen, sunscreen, and more sunscreen while you're out here today, okay? There's plenty in your redhead survival kit. Let me just—"

Declan grabs the tote he gave me, pulls out a small bottle of sunscreen and immediately starts slathering it on my shoulders.

"Buddy, hey," I say softly. "You're freaking me out a little now."

I place my hands over his.

They go still on my shoulders.

He sighs and bows his head. "I'm sorry, Mabel. If you couldn't tell, I'm pretty nervous right now. Meeting you is a big deal for me. And—" He takes a deep breath, then looks deep into my eyes. "I've been meaning to tell you something."

"Care to tell *me* why your hands are on my woman?" A voice I know better than my own heartbeat rings out from a few feet away.

"Wally, hey!" I say. "This is—"

"Declan. Yeah. I figured." He finishes the sentence for me and approaches us with heavy footsteps, his boots scuffing along the cobblestone.

Declan releases his hands from my shoulders and offers Wally a handshake. "Pleasure to finally meet you, man."

"Is it?" Wally does not accept the handshake, just stares Declan down.

"Yeah," Declan says. "It really is."

Wally wraps an arm around me in response. It should make me feel warm, but I get a chill instead.

"Ooooh." I shudder. "The way you called me your woman just now reminded me of a scene in one of Calliope's books where a T-Rex and a Coelophysis were making love—a challenge for them because of their size difference and the fact that the T-Rex couldn't grab her the way he wanted to with those cute stubby arms of his. But anyway, in the scene, they're doing the darnedest to make love, and the T-Rex keeps growling 'Mine. Mine. You're mine' with every single thrust. I was struck then—and now—by something. As women, we're told we're not supposed to like that possessive male stuff, but I'll be damned if that energy didn't make me feel all giggly and tingly inside."

"That sounds like a Tracy Triassic plot," Declan says.

"It is! And shoot, you're right, it's *Tracy*, not Calliope. Tracy." I smack my forehead. "Wait. You read her books?"

"I do! They're awesome! Wait," he says. "You're *friends* with Tracy Triassic?"

"I am! But please forget I slipped and told you her real name!"

"Zipping my lips and throwing away the key, lady!" Declan mimes the action while he says it.

"Phew!" I say.

Wally's gaze ping pongs from me to Declan and back again as the giddy energy between us keeps escalating.

"Miss McGonigiggle, are you telling me that we both have red hair?"

"Yes!"

"We both love Cap'n Crunch Berries cereal?"

"Yes!"

"We both sleep with one sock on and one sock off and we both think dino romance is the bomb dot com?"

"Yes!"

"Ohmygodit'slikewe'rethesameperson!" Declan and I squeal in unison and jump up and down like happy, totally in sync idiots.

When we stop bouncing, Wally is super steady and staring at us both.

"Alright," he says, his voice deeper than I've ever heard it. "What the hell is happening here?"

I look at Declan, then back at Wally, feeling panicked for some reason. "I'm—I'm not sure what—Wally, I promise, there's nothing you need to—" I stumble over my words and can't get a full thought out.

"Mabel?" Declan says. "I got this."

"Oh you *got* this, do you?" Wally says sarcastically.

"I do."

Declan stands his ground, but there's a pink flush rising to his cheeks. It's one of the downfalls to being a redhead. Our fair complexion shows what we're feeling every single time.

Declan is shook.

"I see why you're confused, man," he continues. "And I get why you feel threatened."

"Threatened?" Wally scoffs. "No. I'm not *threatened*. I'm also not confused. You've been creeping on Mabel for months, essentially stalking her, and now—"

"No," Declan says emphatically. "It's not what you think. I'm not Mabel's stalker."

"Then what are you?" Wally asks.

Declan places a hand back on my shoulder.

"I'm her brother."

Chapter Four

WALLY

"Alright, D-Clan. You dropped one hell of a bomb earlier today. Time to talk, pal."

We're in a bar aptly—and annoyingly—called *Bar*. We're sitting across from this Declan guy, who has an awful lot of explaining to do.

"Walla-Walla?" Mabel rests a hand on my forearm. "I know I said I was turned on by the whole alpha guy thing this afternoon, but can we try to simmer down now? And can we pronounce Declan's name correctly? I really want as little drama as possible."

"That's what I want too," Declan says. "I'm truly sorry about before. I didn't mean to blurt out news like that and then run. I had a lot of survival kits to distribute, and I knew if I got into the full story right then, a whole lotta redheads would be without their sunscreen and left-handed scissors."

I sip my beer and place it back on the table harder than necessary. "What?"

"People with red hair are more likely to be left-handed," he explains. "And of course, we all know redheads need to be careful in the sun."

"Surrrrrrre," I say, wishing this guy would cut to the chase already. But I'm trying to honor Mabel's wishes and keep my cool.

"What's that about?" Mabel asks lightheartedly. "The whole 'redheads are more likely to be left-handed' thing?"

"It's because both are recessive traits and recessive traits often come in pairs," Declan says.

"Oh wow! I didn't realize that, and I *am* a left-handed redhead!" she says proudly.

"Me too!" he gleefully responds.

They high-five across the table.

I feel like I've entered an alternate universe.

"Gosh, until now, I never linked my left-handedness to my redheadedness." Mabel says. "I always attributed it to my presidential qualities, of which I have many. Wouldn't you agree, Wally?"

She flashes that beautiful smile and snuggles closer to me.

"So many presidential qualities." I smile back and give her a squeeze.

Trying to be a good sport, here. I really am.

Mabel takes a sip of her cider and continues, "Declan, did you know that eight out of the forty-six presidents we've had so far were left-handed? That's seventeen percent! My friend Louise is super into *Jeopardy*. She told me that tidbit."

"Did your friend Louise tell you who the left-handed presidents are?" he asks.

"She did, actually!" Mabel starts counting off on her fingers. "Garfield, Hoover, Truman, Ford, Reagan, Bush—that's H. W. not W.—Clinton and Obama. Haha, why do I remember that?" She gasps. "Wait a damn second! Were any of those POTUSes redheads too?"

"Unfortunately, no. The double recessive trait thing doesn't play here. Our redheaded and *right-handed* presidents were Kennedy, Coolidge, Taft, Hayes, Van Buren, Jackson and Jefferson."

Oh my God, make it stop.

"Are you sure Jefferson was a redhead?" Mabel's eyebrows draw together.

"Yup!" Declan says. "History remembers him with that curly gray wig, but underneath was a whole lotta red."

"Wow. Who knew?" Mabel happily knocks back more cider.

"Well. Prepare to have your mind blown even more, lady."

Mabel leans forward, completely engaged in this inane discussion. "Blow me, baby!" She pauses. "That sounded weird. You know what I meant. Gimme the scoop!"

Seriously, kill me now.

Declan lowers his voice like he has a really cool secret. "While Jefferson wasn't technically a left-handed redhead, he did demonstrate left-handed *ability*."

"What do you mean?" Mabel asks excitedly.

"He was originally right-handed, but after an injury to his right wrist, he became ambidextrous. He was redheaded by birth, but left-handed by default, so I don't think we can actually count him as an original left-handed redhead, but some would argue that—"

"OH MY GOD, WILL YOU SHUT UP!?"

Dammit.

I've officially lost my cool.

The two possibly related left-handed redheads stare at me in silence.

"Wally," Mabel says softly, clearly shocked by my outburst.

I sigh. "Sorry, Mabes, but this guy drops the news this afternoon that he's your supposed biological brother, and instead of getting to the bottom of that discussion, we're ass-deep in a dissertation about the hair color and scissor habits of US presidents? I mean, what world am I living in right now?"

"Scissor habits." Mabel snorts. "That sounds naughty."

"It does not!" I shout.

Declan laughs and says under his breath, "It sort of does."

I take another swig of my beer to gather my emotional bearings.

I clear my throat.

"I apologize for yelling." I turn toward my girlfriend and speak only to her. "Mabey Baby, I don't mean to be harsh here, but this revelation will likely have a significant impact on your life. Shouldn't we stop joking around and figure it all out?"

She mirrors my body language and whispers back, "You're right. We should. I'm just... I'm—" Her eyes glisten. "I think I'm freaked out about it all, you know? I mean, after everything that went down two years ago, how many family surprises can one girl handle?"

"That's totally understandable. I'm not sure if you've noticed, though." I stroke her cheek. "You're Mabel fucking McGonigle. You can handle anything. And besides, you have me this time. We'll get through this like we do everything. Together."

The tears that glistened in her eyes a moment ago spill over, but it's clear they're happy tears.

She dives into my arms. "I love you so much."

"Love you more, beautiful," I whisper and hold her tight.

"Declan?" she says. "Do you mind if I make out with my boyfriend for a minute? It could get pretty graphic."

"Oh, uh. Sure. That's fine. I'll just—"

He turns so he's facing the wood paneling behind him.

"Thank you, sir," she says, then puts her full attention on me. "Here I come, big guy."

"Thanks for the warning." I laugh.

She gives me that adorable disaster of a wink again, then kisses the hell outta me until we're both breathless.

She has me wishing I could take her back to our flat immediately. But we really do have to deal with this. We finish the kiss. I smooth her hair.

"All good?" I ask.

"All good, yes. Declan, you can turn back around."

"You two are a really cute couple." Declan tips his glass up to us. "I'm happy for you."

"Thank you," Mabel beams.

I nod in acknowledgment, but this guy isn't off the hook with me yet.

He must read that on my face because he sighs and says, "So. I'll tell you everything I know, and you should feel free to ask me whatever questions you have because I'm sure you'll have a lot and—"

Mabel raises her hand. "Can I say something first?"

"Of course, yeah," Declan says.

"A part of me is freaking out, but whew! An even bigger part of me is freaking relieved! Because I was so confused! I had all these strong feelings for you—that were definitely *not* pants feelings— which was a good thing because I am a committed woman. But they were stronger than friendship feelings, and I had no idea what they could mean."

"Pants feelings?" Declan looks at me for an explanation.

"Like the kind she has for me," I say and sip my beer.

"Exactly." Mabel nods. "Like a moment ago, when I kissed Wally? I had pants feelings out the wazoo! But never with you."

Declan smiles. "Because I'm your brother."

Happy tears well in Mabel's eyes again. "Because you're my brother."

"Ahhhhhhhhhhhh!" Declan and Mabel squeal in unison, then leap out of their seats and do that synchronized jumping-hugging thing again.

"I already love you!" Mabel shouts.

"I already love you too!" he shouts back.

Mabel stops bouncing and puts him at arm's length. "But like in a brotherly way, right? I'm just checking one more time because, you know, you're my brother."

"I think we've sufficiently established that neither of you has incestuous intent. Can we move on to some facts and explanations please?" I ask.

Declan gives me a thumbs-up and takes his seat.

I open my arms for Mabel to join me back on our side of the booth.

Once everyone's settled, I say, "How did you figure out your connection in the first place?"

"Well, I've always been a curious person," Declan says. "So when everyone was doing those ancestry DNA kits a while back, I thought, 'why the hell not?'"

"I did one too!" Mabel says.

"I know," Declan says. "That's how I found you. A 'Mabel McGonigle' popped up as my half sibling, sharing twenty-five percent of my DNA. After that, a quick online search of your name led me to your YouTube show. When I saw you, I knew it was you. The resemblance to my family was undeniable. I sent you messages through the testing portal, but you never opened them."

"Mabes, you never told me you did the ancestry thing."

I'm sure I sound hurt when I say it.

I thought we told each other everything.

"I know. I'm sorry. But that's because I only *sort of* did it," she says.

"How do you only sort of do a DNA test?" I huff.

"I signed up in a tizzy when everything went down with my parents, sort of as a subtle screw you to them. Because what else were they hiding from me, ya know? I did the swab thingy and sent it in, but then when it came time to look at the results, I just...

didn't. I couldn't."

"Why not?"

"Because I was still dealing with Tina and Chloe and my parents and... Seriously, why does this keep happening to me?!"

"This keeps happening to you?" Declan's head cocks to the side.

"Two years ago, she found out she has a sister on her mom's side," I explain. "She didn't *know* her mom was her mom. She actually thought her *grandmom* was her mom and—"

"Whoa, whoa, whoa. Not sure I'm following. Can we back up a bit?" Declan says, then signals our server for another round.

"I got this, Walla-Walla Bing Bang." Mabel knocks back the rest of her drink, then launches into a rapid-fire recap of her family drama. "Okay, so my whole life, my parents—especially my dad—have been super overprotective. No sleepovers. No family friends. No fun. As Wally likes to say, I was 'sheltered as shit.' My parents had this strained relationship with my 'Aunt Tina'—that's what they always called her—and I could never understand why. Turns out, Tina is actually their daughter and *my* mom. Yup, the people I always thought were my parents are biologically my grandparents." She pauses a second to gauge whether or not Declan is still with her. He nods and encourages her to continue. "Okay, so Tina had me when she was pretty young. They shamed her blah, blah, blah..."

"'They shamed her blah, blah, blah?'" I laugh at her description of past events.

"What?" Mabel lightly shoves me. "I'm not going into details here. I'm just giving him the gist." She puts her attention back on Declan. "They eventually tell her they will take care of me and raise me as their own so she can go to school and have a life blah, blah, blah, which *sounds* like a generous, loving thing to do, right? Eeeng!" She makes the buzzer sound you hear on game shows when a contestant gets something wrong. "They get all weird and secretive about it, all 'nobody can ever know.' Fast-forward to when I was nine-ish. Tina was older and in a better place. She wanted me to be her daughter for real. My dad lost his mind, cut her off completely, and doubled down on his lies until he had a heart attack and almost died."

"Wow," Declan says.

"Did I hit all the relevant plot points?" she asks me.

"You wanna tell him about Chloe?" I say.

"Yes. Yesyesyes, of course."

Our server delivers another round of drinks. Mabel thanks her and takes a few generous gulps.

"Hey baby, maybe we should slow it down a bit?" I suggest.

"With the story or the cider?" she asks, a bit breathless.

"The cider."

"Eh, don't be a nincompoop. I'm on a roll here."

A nincompoop. Geez.

She takes another gulp and continues the story. "Two summers ago, this girl gets a counselor-in-training job at the camp where I was working—the same place where I met and fell in love with this fella." She juts her thumb to me. "Turns out she was my half sister, Chloe. Though we leave off the half part. You can't love someone halfway. She applied for the job in the first place after doing some detective work in her own house. She had a hunch we were related and wanted to solve the mystery. So she discovered the truth, spilled the beans, everyone's lies were exposed, and now I have a sister who freaking rules. Wow, my life sounds really interesting when I let it all hang out like that, doesn't it? But seriously, Chloe is the greatest gift that came out of the whole situation. After a lifetime of feeling lonely and disconnected from my family, now I have a sister! And gosh, a brother too! I shouldn't have weenied out on the testing site results."

Mabel's eyes get misty as she takes Declan's hand across the table.

"I could have found you so much sooner." She sniffs.

"We've found each other now. That's all that matters."

"Yeah," Mabel says wistfully.

"I do have to make one correction to your story, though," Declan says.

"What do you mean?" I feel myself getting defensive all over again. "That's her story. What is there to correct?"

"You don't just have one sister, Mabel."

"I don't?"

"No. You have six."

Chapter Five

MABEL

"Six sisters??? Holy shit!" I shout, then look around the busy bar. "Excuse my language, everybody. I'm just motherfucking shocked over here."

"No excusing necessary," Declan says. "This is definitely a 'holy shit' moment. I look forward to meeting Chloe someday, but, yeah, your other five sisters will be here any minute."

My hands grip the edge of the wooden table and try to get a hold on my breathing. "I think my head just flew out of my butt."

"That sounds like a medical problem you might want to get checked out." Declan chuckles.

"Wait. *Why* will they all be here any minute?" I ask, feeling like I'm going to hyperventilate.

"Remember when I said I sing with my family?"

"Right, yes!"

"Well, our set starts in half an hour. But to answer your unspoken question, yes, I told them about you. And they are so excited to meet you."

Hey, Wally." I dig my nails into my boyfriend's arm so hard he flinches. "Declan has a band with his sisters."

"And my dad," Declan says.

"AND HIS DAD! Hahahaha! Oh my God, I'm going to meet my birth dad!!"

"Mabes, you okay?" Wally dislodges my nails from his forearm and threads his fingers through mine.

"Totally. This is not a big deal. I'm just finally going to meet Porkrind!"

"Sorry, who's *Porkrind*?" Declan's brow furrows.

"Our dad!" I say.

"Our dad's name is Matthew," he corrects.

"Huh. My birth mom told me she had a one-night stand with a redheaded guy named Porkrind twenty-six years ago. He lived in South Philly. She never told him about me. She gave me the last phone number she had for him, but it was disconnected when I got the guts to try him on it."

"Well, yeah, twenty-six years later, I would assume it would be! Let me text him and see if anyone called him Porkrind in the past."

Declan fires off a text while I continue, "After the failed phone call, I googled 'a man named Porkrind,' but all I found were animated pictures of a muscular pig with an eyepatch. At the time, it felt like a sign to leave things well enough alone, ya know? What if he wasn't a good guy? Tina couldn't tell me much about him. She never knew his real name." I snort in anticipation of the joke I'm about to make. "Seems they seven kipped the talking and went right to the porking. Hahahaha. I kill me, sometimes."

"I'm surprised you can laugh about this," Wally says, a hand on my thigh.

"When your whole life has been a lie, you can laugh, or you can cry, right?" I look into his eyes and fight the urge to let loose a snotty sob fest right here and now.

I'm so overwhelmed.

And when I'm overwhelmed, I make jokes.

"Hey Declan, does Papa Porkrind know he gave Tina the baby gravy and put a punk in da trunk? Does he know because of all dat internal fluff he got her up the duff? That thanks to his chub, she joined the pudding club?"

"Who are you right now?" Wally whispers in my ear.

"That's just it, Wally." I sniffle. "I have no idea who I am anymore! Two years ago, my world was so small. Now it feels like it's expanding every second. I have Chloe and Tina and Calliope and *Lou*. Ralph and James and, most importantly, *you*. I thought I had no siblings, and suddenly, I have *seven*? I can't tell if I'm in hell or some kind of *heaven*."

"Is she rhyming?" Declan asks Wally.

"Yeah. She does that sometimes when she's emotional."

"Got it. And where did all that filth come from a moment ago? That was... impressive. And... unnecessarily creative."

I chime in to explain that one. "Sometimes when Calliope—sorry, *Tracy*—brainstorms scenes for her books, Louise and I hop on Urban Thesaurus and serve her up with some synonyms. After writing twenty romance books, there are only so many ways left to describe sex."

"You're a shoo-in for the family band," Declan says.

"Is it a family *sex* band?" Wally asks, a look of horror on his face.

"Of course not. Poor transition on my part. We're a redheaded family improvisational singing band."

"Shit. That sounds even worse." Wally takes a swig of his beer.

"To answer your question, Mabel. Yes. He knows about you. *Now.* I told him last night. But that was the first he'd heard of it."

Was he happy?

Upset?

Angry?

Does he want anything to do with me?

I feel my breathing ratcheting up. I have no idea what to say. What to do. So I do the only logical thing I can think of.

"Speaking of bands..."

"Mabel..." Wally says in his warning voice.

"Wally was in a band back in the day! It was way before he met me."

"Oh yeah?" Declan says. "What kind of band?"

"Heavy metal!"

Wally gives me a look.

I know he doesn't love talking about this part of his life, but damn, I'll do anything to distract from the fact that at any moment my birth dad could walk through that door. Even selling out the love of my life.

"They were called The Poison Puppetmasters," I continue. "It was his college band. They were kind of like that old NSYNC boy band video where they were dancing on puppet strings, but Wally and his Poison Puppetmasters were way scarier and screamed so much more. Oh! And they threatened to choke the audience with their puppet ropes."

"Wow!" Declan looks wary of Wally now.

"It was a theatrical gimmick." Wally shrugs. "Just kids being dumb."

"It wasn't dumb, though!" I argue. "I've said it before, and I'll say it again. The way you screamed the lyrics in that movie monster voice was amazing! And arousing!"

"I deeply regret ever showing you that old footage."

"I don't! In fact, I spend way too much of my life wishing and hoping for the day you'll sing to me that way. When you'll be like, 'MABEL! I LOVE YOU! I LOVE YOU SO MUCH! YOU ARE THE GIRL THAT I LOVE TO TOUCH! RAAAAAAAAAAAHHHH!'"

Wally tries his best not to laugh, but I see that smile in his eyes. He'll never admit it, but he's powerless when I do my Poison Puppetmaster impression.

"That was a sick metal voice, Mabes!" Declan laughs his butt off. "Man, is there anything you can't do?"

That's my cue to take it even further.

"NO! THERE ISN'T! I CAN DO IT ALLLLLL! I'LL TEACH YOU ABOUT BUGS! AND BEES! HOW TO BE A NUDIST IN THE FALL!!"

That one does Wally in, and the brightest smile spreads across his face, which only makes me want to keep going. But as I continue, the joy in my belly quickly turns sour and strange.

"PEOPLE LIE TO ME ALL THE FUCKING TIME! BUT I SMILE AND SMILE AND TELL EVERYONE I'M FINE! MY BIRTH DAD IS PORKRIND! HE HAD AN AWFUL PERM! BUT HE'S FATHERED SEVEN CHILDREN! HE MUST HAVE SUPER SPERM!"

I am so lost in my ridiculous, sad moment, that I don't realize two things.

One: I'm crying.

Two: We have company.

I wipe my tears and whip my head in the direction Wally and Declan are now staring.

Five beautiful redheaded young women stand there with eyes wide and mouths open.

Beside them is an older man with a sweet face and a gentle smile.

I look just like him.

Chapter Six

WALLY

Mabel is completely frozen.

I stroke her hair and whisper, "Wally and Mabel sitting in a tree. We get through everything together, right?"

"Right," she whispers back, but her eyes never leave the redheaded crew assembled in front of us.

Just when it feels like no one is going to speak, and we'll be at the center of this 9-person stand-off forever, the older gentleman, Matthew, clears his throat.

"I just got your text, Dec. They called me Porkrind back then because of this guy right here."

He tugs on his left ear. It's misshapen, kind of gnarled and crunchy looking, like... well, like a pork rind.

"A gift from my jujitsu days." He attempts a wink.

What do you know, it's the same bizarre open-mouthed two-eyed blink that Mabel does.

Genetics are wild.

"I'm sorry about your ear, sir. And I'm sure your perm was lovely," Mabel breathes. "I shouldn't have said that. Also, your sperm is *your* business. Whether it's super or not is not for me to say. Perm and sperm just fit together so perfectly, it felt like a missed opportunity if I didn't embrace that particular rhyme."

"I understand completely," he says with a smile, then turns to Declan. "She's a shoo-in for the family band."

"That's what I said!" Declan laughs, then softens his voice. "I'm sure you've already put it together, Dad, but this is Mabel. Your daughter."

"My daughter," the man repeats, his eyes welling with tears.

"It's a girl! Congratulations!" Mabel raises the roof, then gives us all spirit fingers. Everyone silently smiles. Her eyes dart between her dad and the five young women standing in front of us. "Looks like you're all set with daughters, though, huh? Hahaha." Her cheeks flush with pink. "Okay, listen, I don't want to intrude on this cool family thing you've got going on, so I'm just— I'm gonna go." She grabs her purse and tugs on my shirtsleeve. "Let's head out, Walla-Walla, and give these people some—"

"Mabel," Matthew interrupts. "You could never intrude. I know this feels complicated right now, but... this is thrilling news. I'm— *we're* thrilled." A tear spills down his cheek. He makes no attempt to wipe it away. "And I'd really like to talk to you. Think I could sit down with you for a few minutes?"

"Sure, Porkrind. I mean Dad. I mean Matthew."

He laughs. "You can call me whatever makes you most comfortable." He turns to his other five daughters, three of which have to be identical triplets. They look ready to burst, like they took a collective inhale when they entered and haven't breathed out since. "Girls? Your restraint thus far has been commendable. Think you can say hi without scaring her?"

That's when all happy hell breaks loose, and a stream of questions and teenage squeals ricochet through the bar.

"Mabel, are you staying for the show? How long are you in town? Can I braid your hair? What's it like being a beekeeper? Is it true you don't ever wear clothes?"

Mabel's eyes go wide. "I'm wearing clothes now, aren't I?" She chuckles nervously and looks at Matthew.

He puts his hands up and laughs. "None of my business. Girls, why don't you head back to the greenroom and start the warm- up? Declan and I will be there in just a bit."

The girls sneak in quick hugs with Mabel and a few more frenzied questions before they file out of the main room.

Suddenly, it feels way too quiet for a bustling bar as the four of us stare at each other, wondering what to do next.

"Matthew, sit, will you?" I say. "I haven't officially introduced myself yet." I reach my hand out to him. "I'm Wallace, Mabel's partner."

"In life? Or work?" He shakes my hand and smiles.

"In everything," I say and give Mabel a squeeze.

Matthew takes a seat next to his son and looks back and forth between Mabel and me. "I like that. I like the way you kids talk today, calling your boyfriends and girlfriends *partners*. It's nice."

I laugh and take a sip of my beer. "I'm almost thirty-five years old, sir. Not really a kid anymore."

"You're talking to a man who's approaching sixty. Trust me, you're a kid. And I mean that in the most positive way."

His eyes go wistful.

Mabel blurts, "Wally named his syrup-making company after me. And bought me a tree farm. And built me a house. And a dozen beehives. He's amazing."

"He sure seems it," Matthew says, then smiles at the server who drops off a beer without him even placing an order.

It appears he's a regular here.

He takes a sip, and his face turns serious. "Mabel?"

"Yes?"

"I'm feeling a form of *plaatsvervangende schaamte* right now."

"Do you need a doctor?" Mabel asks hesitantly, clearly having no idea what he means.

Matthew chuckles. "No, I'm fine. *Plaatsvervangende schaamte* is a Dutch phrase. One of those sentiments not easily translated to English. It basically means... that feeling of shame you experience caused by someone else's actions."

Mabel purses her lips but remains silent.

He continues, "What I mean is... I feel shame for the man I used to be, the one who was careless with people's hearts. I wish he'd been more thoughtful and responsible."

"Yeah, you were quite the manwhore back then, huh, Dad?" Declan says.

"Declan!" Matthew scolds. "You're going to use a word like manwhore to describe your father? I thought your generation was against slut shaming."

"We are. *You* brought up the word shame, not me. I just meant, it seems like you were quite a different guy than the one who was married to Mom for over twenty years and raised six kids."

"I was… free with my body as a young man, that's true. I don't regret that per se." He sighs and takes another sip of his beer. "What I do regret is missing out on knowing this wonderful girl all these years."

He rests his open hand on the table in front of Mabel. She surprises me when she places her hand in his and squeezes it.

"It's not really your fault," Mabel says softly. "You didn't know. I'm sure you're pretty mad at Tina for never telling you, huh?"

"Who's Tina?" Matthew asks.

Mabel drops his hand.

"WHO'S TINA? THE WOMAN YOU MANWHORED WITH, DUDE! SHOULDN'T YOU AT LEAST REMEMBER HER NAME!?"

"Whoa, whoa, whoa." I rub a hand up and down Mabel's back.

"I'm sorry for yelling." She rests her head on my shoulder. "This is all just… a lot."

Matthew clears his throat. "Tina. Okay, your mother's name is Tina. My apologies, Mabel. In my mind, she's always been Tinsel."

"Tinsel?" Mabel squeaks.

Declan chimes in, "Seriously, Dad, what the hell were you people up to back then?"

"Let me explain." Matthew ignores Declan's slight and puts his full focus on Mabel. "When I met her, your mother went by Chrissy. Short for Christina, I suppose. The night you were conceived, we were drunk at a Christmas party. I told her she was my Chrissy-mas gift, and I couldn't wait to unwrap her. We made love behind a Christmas tree. I remember pine needles raining down on our naked bodies. But most of all, I remember the tinsel winding its way through her hair, making us both glisten with silver and sex."

It's silent for a moment after that.

"Too much detail, Dad." Declan looks nauseous.

"No, it's fine," Mabel says. "I like the details. It's nice to have details after so long. Tina told me the basics, but she wasn't so… graphic about the details of my conception. I appreciate it, Porkrind."

He smiles and nods. "Tinsel—I mean Tina—is well, then?"

"She is. She's married. Has another daughter. It's a long story I'll let Declan catch you up on, but she wasn't a part of my life for many years. She's good now, though. *We're* good now."

"It sounds like you've been through a lot," Matthew says. "I'm sorry."

"What about you?" Mabel blasts through anything that resembles pity. "Declan said you've been married for over twenty years? That's incredible. Will I meet her tonight? Is she coming to the show?"

Both Declan's and Matthew's eyes go soft at that.

"Our mom passed away six years ago," Declan explains.

"Oh, I'm sorry," Mabel says.

Matthew smiles. "Thank you. You would've loved Irene. And I know she would've loved you. She was the glue that held us all together."

"Give yourself some credit, Dad. You've done a pretty good job of holding us all together yourself." Declan turns to us. "Can you imagine being left a single dad of six kids? Three teenagers and identical twelve-year-old triplets?"

"No," I say. "That sounds like a fucking nightmare."

Mabel nudges me. "I'm sorry. Wally's free with his f-bombs."

"As he should be." Matthew nods approvingly. "But the fucking nightmare turned into something beautiful. Don't get me wrong, I miss Irene every minute of every day. But I take comfort in the fact that my kids are my world, and I know them inside and out. I'm not sure a bond like that would have happened if her death hadn't forced me to step up to the parenting plate in this bigger way."

"That's beautiful," Mabel says, misty-eyed.

"I know you're a grown woman now. We've only just met, and you don't need another father figure. But if you're open to it, I'd love to be a part of your life in whatever way you're comfortable." Matthew pauses and looks at her with hope in his eyes. "There's still time, right?"

Mabel nods and smiles. "There's still time."

They scoot out from their seats and hug each other for a long time.

They pull back from each other, but Matthew continues to face her and hold both of her hands in his.

"It might take me a while to call you Dad," Mabel says. "But I have an idea."

"Hit me."

Mabel slaps him across the face.

"Whoa!" Declan shouts and reaches for his dad.

Matthew holds his cheek and laughs hysterically.

"Oh my God, I'm sorry!" Mabel says. "You didn't mean to *really* hit you, huh?"

"I didn't." Matthew fights to control his laughter. "But I absolutely loved that. I love this girl."

Mabel beams at his declaration.

"So what was your idea?" Matthew asks.

"Oh." She snaps out of her happy stupor. "My friend Louise gave me advice about this exact situation we're in without realizing she was giving it."

"Let's *hear* it." Matthew gives her that two-eyed wink, purposely choosing not to say "hit me" again.

"Well, Louise has had a lot of issues with her dad over the years—" Mabel stops herself. "I'm not saying that I have lots of issues with *you*. I don't really *know* you yet."

"Understood," Matthew says and gestures for her to continue.

"But anyway, Louise said that instead of putting all this pressure on the relationship she has with her father, she's decided to think of him as more of a weird uncle instead. She says that way it doesn't hurt as much when it isn't what she thinks a father/ daughter relationship should be." Mabel shoots finger guns at him and smiles. "You seem awesome, big guy, and I'm super excited to get to know each other. But as we work on that... maybe I could see you as a weird uncle too?"

"Pew pew!" He shoots finger guns back at her.

She startles and laughs.

"Mabel? I'd be honored to be your weird uncle."

"Awesome."

They hug again.

"Dad." Declan rises from his seat and places a hand on Matthew's shoulder. "We should head back and warm up with the girls."

Matthew pulls back from Mabel and gives her an inquisitive look. "Can your weird uncle invite you to join him onstage tonight?"

"Me? What? Why?" She panics.

"First of all…" he says. "It's a family band. And you're family, kid. Second of all, anyone who can weave compelling on-the-spot performance-ready rhymes like you were weaving when I first arrived tonight deserves a chance to be onstage."

"But I'm not a singer! And don't I need to rehearse?"

"We're a musical *improv* group," Declan reminds her. "No rehearsal necessary."

Mabel looks at me for my input. "What do you think, Wally?"

"When you think about it, life is an improvisation, isn't it? We're all making it up as we go."

I don't know where those words come from, but they seem to be the right ones because Mabel's whole beautiful face lights up, and she says, "I'm in! Lead me backstage, boys!"

After giving me a quick kiss and an excited squeal, she links arms with Declan and bounds into the back room.

"We'll see you in the audience, yeah?" Matthew shakes my hand and claps me on the back.

"Yeah, of course. Wouldn't miss it."

"Alright then."

With all the excitement of the past few hours, I almost forgot what I've been carrying in my satchel. Just before Mabel's Dad/ Weird Uncle is out of sight, an idea lands, and I call out to him.

"Hey, Matthew?"

He turns around. "Yeah, kid?"

"Could I run something by you?"

Chapter Seven

MABEL

I'm backstage in the performance area of Bar. By backstage, I mean a small concrete hallway with a bucket full of brown water in the corner and an abundance of cobwebs overhead. What might seem dingy and dirty to others feels magical and brilliant to me.

My family just tripled in size.

It feels like my heart has too.

I'm mid-huddle with my new family, about to go on stage and perform with them, when my phone rings. I immediately know who's on the other end, and I have a deep need to connect with them.

"Oh my gosh, guys," I say to my new bandmates. "I'm so sorry. Do you mind if I take this call real quick? It's Rich Bitch Power Hour back in the States, and I totally forgot to tell my friends I was busy today."

"I don't know what that means, but sure," Declan says. "We're on in five, okay?"

"I'll be less than four," I promise.

The whole crew moves to their places on the tiny stage while I take my phone to the corner and accept the call. Calliope's and Louise's faces appear on-screen.

"My whores!" I shout happily.

"Wait a damn second, McGonigle." Calliope holds up a finger. "I can *possibly* get onboard with the Entreprewhore title for our support group, but calling us straight-up whores as a method of greeting?" She shakes her head. "No. Unacceptable."

"I'm sorry! It just came out. You know I'm flagrantly inappropriate when I'm excited."

Calliope nods. "*Flagrant.* Good word. I never use it in my books, though. Sounds too close to fragrant. I think we can all agree that flagrant excitement and *fragrant* excitement are two very different things. Anyway, why are you so excited?" she asks, then gasps. "Ahhh! Did Wally pro—"

"Shhhhhhhh," Louise scolds her. "Let *Mabel* tell you why she's excited, or you risk ruining a beautiful, once-in-a-lifetime moment for her."

"Did Wally what?" I ask. "And what once-in-a-lifetime moment could Calliope ruin?"

A weird look crosses Calliope's face. "Um. I was just going to ask if Wally *prrrrrrepared* you for the jet lag that will hit you when you fly home in a few days? Because I know this is your first time traveling to Europe, a *once-in-a-lifetime experience*, and I wouldn't want that ruined by unexpected jet lag symptoms."

I shake my head. "He didn't mention that, no."

"Well, I'm glad this came up then! FYI, people are usually fine after the flight there. It's when you return home that the jet lag can kick your ass sideways. So be ready."

"Okaaaay. Thanks for the heads-up! But listen, I'm not sure we *are* heading back in a few days."

"What do you mean?" Louise asks.

"I'm thinking of extending our trip."

"Really? Why?"

I look at the time on my phone. "I only have three minutes left to talk, but guess what? I have a new brother! And a father! And five more sisters! And I'm about to perform onstage with them in a redheaded family musical improvisation band!" I let it all out in one breath.

Calliope scrunches up her nose. "A redheaded family musical improvisation band? That sounds awful."

Louise lets out an exaggerated sigh. "Really, Calliope? That's the most important piece of information you got from what she just said?" She turns her attention back to me. "Mabes, that's some wild shit you just spewed! Quicky. Is this a good thing? A bad thing?"

"It's a great thing!" I say. "My birth mom banged a guy with a perm and a crunchy ear under a Christmas tree, and my life has never been better!"

"Congratulations?" Calliope says, clearly confused.

"Look, I have to go. I'll fill you in as soon as I can, but I had to pick up the phone to tell you that I love you two. Have I ever said that? Because I do. I love the ever-loving shit out of both of you. You're the best friends I've ever had." The emotion rises in my voice. "You became my family when I felt like I didn't have one, and I can't wait to see where life continues to take me with beautiful bitches like you by my side."

"Barf," Calliope says, but she's smiling.

Louise says, "The sentiment Calliope meant to express was, 'We love you too, Mabes. You're a weird little treasure of a human, and life is infinitely better with you in it.'"

"Yes. That. What Louise said." Calliope blows me a kiss. "Have a blast, woman. Fill us in on everything soon."

"I will! Cheerio, buggers!" I pause. "Do the Dutch say cheerio? Or is it just the Brits? Also, how the heck have I never called you buggers before? A bug-loving girl who doesn't call people buggers? Talk about a missed opportunity!"

"Go, weirdo," Calliope says.

"I'm going. I'm going." I laugh and end the call.

I slip my phone into the crate filled with the rest of the band's belongings and am about to step onstage when I hear a familiar voice.

"Hey, Mabel Again. They let me back here to wish you good luck." I rush into Wally's arms.

"After all this time, you're still calling me Mabel Again?"

"I said it once, and I'll say it until the end of time, 'What on earth could be better than Mabel Again and again and again?'"

"Always such a romantic." I smile and plant a kiss on his lips. "Hey, Declan said you asked to talk to Matthew before he came backstage?"

"I did indeed."

"What did you talk about?"

"That's between me and Porkrind, ma'am."

I cock my head to the side. "You weren't weird, were you? You didn't threaten him or anything?"

Wally laughs. "*Threaten* him? Who do you think you're talking to? I'm the peaceful, tree-loving guy who once told you I made a pact with Nature to release my ego and always celebrate the everyday magic in life."

"You're also the guy who used to only communicate in grunts and frightened children to the point they created urban legends about you. And you creeped me out so much I assumed you buried dead bodies behind your shack by the lake."

"That's fair." He pauses and cups my cheek. "Well, love can change a person. Can't it?"

"It sure can." I nuzzle my cheek deeper into his hand, then kiss his palm. "Love you, Walla-Walla."

"Love you too, Mabey Baby."

We part ways, but I turn when he calls after me.

"Hey, Mabes? Just checking. Were you really *creeped out* by me in our early days? Or were you aroused?"

"I was... creepily aroused." I laugh, and so does he. "Yeah, it was a confusing time for me."

"Knock 'em dead out there," he says, then exits the hall and heads toward his seat in the audience.

I close my eyes and take a deep breath.

What the heck have I signed myself up for?

Declan pokes his head into the hall. "You ready, sis?"

As ready as I'll ever be.

I step onto the stage right between Declan and Matthew. They each take a hand and give me a squeeze.

"Remember what we told you, kid," Matthew says. "You can't do anything wrong. Improvisation is a group effort. Whatever you come up with, your team will back you up."

That's exactly right," Declan agrees. "We're in this together. And fun is the name of the game. We'll introduce you, take votes on a theme, and we'll launch into your intro song."

The oldest of my new sisters, Lily, starts playing a series of rhythmic chords on the piano to signal the start of the show. Poppy, the next in line, has a fiddle on her shoulder and a bow in hand. And the triplets, Daisy, Sage, and Marigold, make up the percussion section with a tambourine, a triangle, and a small hand drum.

Yes, all my new sisters are named after flowers.

Then there's me.

Mabel.

There's no Mabel flower out there—at least as far as I know.

But then I realize the new significance of my *middle* name. It's just a coincidence of course. The parents who raised me couldn't have known how giving me that name would help me weave into the tapestry of this more expansive family twenty-six years later. Still, the synchronicity makes me smile.

A wave of belonging washes over me like I've never felt before.

"Can we nix the third possible theme for my intro song and add a different one instead?" I ask Declan.

"Sure. What is it?"

I whisper it in his ear just as the flimsy mothball-eaten red curtain rises. My eyes go wide at the sight of the audience. There's gotta be over a hundred people squeezed into this room. They're shoulder to shoulder, lifting their beers up to us in welcome.

Poppy finishes playing a rousing opening on the fiddle as Matthew takes the microphone at center stage.

"Good evening and Goedenavond, friends! It's our family's favorite week of the whole year, and tonight is a particularly special show. You may be wondering who this young woman is to my left. Well, I'll let her tell you. Take it away, Mabel."

"Take what away?" I whisper.

"He means start," Declan whispers back. "Start the song."

Matthew places a warm hand on my shoulder as I switch places with him and speak directly into the microphone.

"Hi, everybody." Microphone feedback screeches through the room. I take a slight step back. "Ah. Sorry. I'm new to this." I pause and consider what I just said. "But aren't we all new to this? To life? I mean, when you really think about it? We're all making it up as we go along, right?"

I spot Wally in the center of the audience.

He mouths, "I love you."

Those words and that twinkle in his eye give me all the

encouragement I need to dive in.

I approach the microphone with a bit more finesse this time.

"I've only been in your awesome country for a few days, but I want to thank you for how friendly and welcoming you are. One thing I particularly love is how you're not afraid to be a little bit extra. Take the Dutch language, for example. I was told it is one of the easier languages for English speakers to pick up, but I'm not so sure about that! Come on, all those compound nouns you guys do? This morning, I learned the word that means 'preparation activities for a children's carnival procession.' It's *kindercarnavalsoptochtvoorbereidingswerkzaamhedenplan.* I mean, whaaaaaat?"

I check with a nice-looking lady in the front row. "How was my pronunciation just now? Terrible?"

The lady winces and shakes her head, telling me all I need to know. I butchered that one good.

"Sorry about that. My point is, the Dutch take their time. They take up space. And that's refreshing! Especially for young women! Who cares if a word takes over five minutes to say? There's a lotta double vowels to get out there in your language! Oh, and here's another great example of you all being that little bit extra: double dutch. The rest of the world was cool with one jump rope, but not you guys! You were like, 'nah, gimme two!'"

"Is this a comedy set or a music hour?" a random redheaded guy in the back row shouts.

Matthew clears his throat and gives me an encouraging nod.

"Right. Time to sing." I shimmy my shoulders and let out an operatictrilltotestmyvocalreadiness. "Ooooooooooaaaaaaaaaah! This girl is ready to rock." I hesitate. "I just have to say one more quick thing, and then I'll sing, I promise. I love it here. Thank you for becoming an instant home away from home for me. As you're about to find out, I'm a little bit extra too, just like you."

I pause, then count like the international rock star I apparently am.

"A one! A two! A one, two, three, four!"

Wholesome piano, fiddle, and drumming commence.

"Alright, friends!" Declan shouts over the music. "You know the drill! For our opening number, we give you three topics. The one that gets the loudest vote is the winner. We're throwing Mabel into the deep end right away as our first soloist tonight, so be nice to her, okay?" He stands behind me and places his hands on my shoulders while continuing to address the audience. "In no particular order, the topics Mabel can confidently improvise on are... Bugs!" The audience claps half-heartedly. "Nudity!" The applause is a bit heartier this time, with a few male "woos!" from the back. "And... flowers!"

The place goes nuts.

"Wow!" I turn and shout to Declan. "The Dutch really love their flowers, huh?"

"We're called The Land of Flowers for a reason!" he shouts back.

Matthew gives the crowd the signal to simmer down while my sisters in the band kick the music into a higher gear.

That's my cue.

I close my eyes, connect to my breathing, and sing whatever comes to my brain in this red-hot minute.

> *Hey all you Dutchies!*
> *I hope we can be pals.*
> *I really love your tulips.*
> *And your cool-as-heck canals.*

> *I came here to sell honey*
> *See the country and feel free*
> *What I got was a new brother*
> *And a whole new family*

So far so good.

I point at the band to signal the start of the chorus I'm about to pull out of my butt. They're right there with me, swelling their instruments, and scatting and vocalizing in support. In total sync. It's so darn trippy.

> *Flowers need to grow*
> *Flowers need to grow*
> *We need water, love, and sun*
> *To let our blessings fucking flow!*

Oh, I'm really cooking now. It's like some wild creative force starts pulsing through me and there's no turning back. It demands that I sing my truth out loud. Unfiltered. Raw and real.

Matthew is my daddy
He porked my mom under a tree.
Nine months later
She sprouted little baby me.

I was chubby and wubby
A cutie wootie pie.
But my parents couldn't raise me
I grew up stunted with a lie.

Twenty-four years later
My world turned upside down
My roots were all uplifted
The dirt they spilled was dark and brown

"Oooooooh," I add in a shudder for added drama, then signal the chorus again.

Declan, Matthew, and the girls add new musical flourishes this time, building on what we discovered together before.

Flowers need to grow
Flowers need to grow
We need water, love, and sun
To let our blessings fucking flow!

This feels like the right time for a bridge, right?

Of course! Every great song has a great bridge.

My body moves without my conscious permission. Before I know it, I'm busting out these smooth hip sways and even smoother rhymes. The vibe turns all sorts of sensual.

Is this weird behavior for a family band? Maybe. But the spirit is moving me, and there ain't no way I'm going to stop now.

I zero in on Wally in the center row, and my cheeks warm.

I met my man.
He was not a fan.
Falling in love with me
Was not his plan
But after funnilingus in the shower
An outdoor sexy power hour
He became my guy
My soul learned how to fly

My heart planted in his, and I finally knew how to flowerrrrrrrr!
That creative energy pulsing in me tells me to bring things home with that realization I had backstage.

My new sisters are Lily and Poppy
Daisy, Sage, and Marigold.
I didn't get to meet them
Until I was twenty-six years old.

I was sad my name was Mabel.
Not a flower name at all
But my middle name is Rose
Some roses grow to eight feet tall.

One more chorus should do the trick.
I don't even need to signal my family this time. They know what's coming next.

Flowers need to grow
Flowers need to grow
We need water, love, and sun
To let our blessings fucking flow!

When Declan and the girls gave me tips before we started, they said it's up to the soloist to determine when the song is over. I thought that last chorus would be my grand finish, but when I catch a misty-eyed Wally in the audience, brushing away a tear, an idea for one last verse washes over me and pours out of me like water.

I'm unbelievably happy
My life feels so complete.
When I feel this freaking joyful
I want to suck at that man's teat.

His name is Wally Bieber.
He's my sexy Wally Bee.
Please whip out your stinger
And pollinate me.

The audience collectively gasps.
It spurs me on.

Pollinate me. Puh-puh-puh-pollinate me.
Pollinate me. Puh-puh-puh-pollinate me.
Pollinate me. Puh-puh-puh-

Declan unexpectedly cuts me off. "Okay! That was—Wow! What a debut, huh?"

He takes my hand. I look up at him, bleary-eyed as he pulls me to my feet. Until that moment, I didn't realize I was on the floor.

Was I *gyrating* on the floor?

The audience is silent, and quite a few mouths hang open.

They look as dazed as I feel.

"I warned you I was a little extra, right?" I say softly into the microphone.

Wally starts a slow clap.

The audience gradually joins him. Soon hoots and hollers add to the mix until the room fully erupts in enthusiastic applause.

I curtsey and place my hands over my heart.

What a rush.

"We want more! We want more!" the crowd chants.

"You liked that, huh?" Declan sounds surprised. "We usually perform more wholesome, family-friendly fare, but hey! That's great!" He squints as he scans the room. "We're all eighteen and older here, right?"

They cheer.

Declan leans closer to me and speaks so only I can hear. "That was incredible. I am very proud of you. Are we in agreement, though, that there will be no actual public pollination onstage? Because that would definitely cross some lines and get us kicked out."

I give him a serious thumbs-up.

Matthew moves us aside and takes center stage, surprising us both. "Folks, if you liked that, then you're going to love what's coming next! We have another special guest with us tonight."

We do? Suddenly, I'm not feeling so special.

"Dad, what are you doing?" Declan asks.

Matthew continues to speak into the microphone. "It's time to hear from The Pollinator himself. Wally B? Would you join us onstage?"

Chapter Eight

WALLY

When I hop onto the wooden platform, Mabel dives immediately into my arms. "What are you doing up here?"

"That was quite a performance, beautiful." I ignore her question for the time being and inhale the scent of her apple honey shampoo.

She's still squeezing me tight. "Was it okay? It felt right at the moment, but now I'm having a hard time looking audience members directly in the eye."

"Think it's because you repeatedly invited me to *pollinate* you in front of them?"

"Maybe?" she says. "It was the wildest thing, Walla-Walla. It was like the creative energy of the Universe grabbed me by the balls and wouldn't let me go. It felt like we made a vow: that as long as I agreed to serve as her musical bitch, she'd stay embedded in my crotch hairs and serve *me* with sweet, sweet rhymes."

"What?" I tilt my head in wonder of this woman.

"Hey, guys?" Declan taps me on the shoulder and whispers, "The microphone is picking up everything you're saying. Also... we really should continue with the show."

For the first time since I climbed onstage, I take in the hundred or so people in the audience sipping their beers and waiting patiently for the next act. It feels like there are so many more of them when you're standing up here.

Matthew directs Mabel's attention to an empty front-row seat. "For you, dear."

"I don't get it." Mabel looks at him, then back at me. "What's going on?"

Matthew just smiles, then gathers Declan and the rest of the band in a family huddle to get them onboard.

I take Mabel's hand and guide her down to the floor. "I have an announcement to make, and I think you should be sitting when I make it."

"Oh my God, you're not my brother too, are you?"

"Of course not."

"Okay good." She sighs. "Because that would be a problem."

"It sure as fuck would."

I get her settled in the front-row seat that an audience member kindly vacated for me when I told him my plan.

"Because now that you're mine," Mabel continues, "I don't think I could ever let you go, ya know? We'd have to be like the people you see on those old-school trashy talk shows. You know the folks I'm talking about? The ones who were unintentionally incestuous? And then after the DNA reveal that they are in fact related, they're just too in love to stop what they're doing, so they double down on their situation and say, 'I'm sleeping with my brother, and it's none-a-ya damn business!'"

Titters spread across the crowd.

"Mabes?" I lean down and speak softly to her. "Can we resume this discussion later? Or actually, maybe we can drop it completely? I'm not your brother. Promise."

"Phew!" She pulls me to her by the back of my neck and kisses me deeply.

As I make my way back onstage, an older gentleman gives me the stink eye.

"I swear I'm not her brother," I mumble again, in disbelief that these are the words I'm saying right before I propose marriage.

Matthew announces, "Alright friends, let's welcome back to the stage... Wally Bee The Pollinator!"

I lean into the mic. "Just, um. Wallace or Wally will be fine," I say politely.

Declan and the girls start a musical vamp behind me. My heart rate picks up speed.

I turn my back to crowd and try to get myself under control.

"You okay, kid? Anything I can do?" Matthew says in a hushed voice, tambourine in hand.

"I'm fine, but yeah, there is something you can do. Could you refrain from calling me The Pollinator? For all intents and purposes, you're my father-in-law." I shrug. "Feels kinda weird."

"Oh sure, sure. Sorry about that. Sometimes performance energy gets the better of me. Did you bring the stuff?" He smacks me on the butt with the tambourine.

"The *stuff*? This is a proposal, Matt, not a drug deal." I rub my ass where he smacked me. "If you're asking if I have the ring, then yeah. I have the ring."

He smiles so wide that I can see the fillings in his back teeth.

"Then let's do this thing."

Matthew gives Declan and the girls the signal to kick the music into higher gear. He turns me by the shoulders and shoves me gently toward the mic.

I address the audience. "Let it be known that the nerves I'm currently exhibiting have nothing to do with doubts about what I'm about to ask, and everything to do with the *way* I'm about to ask it."

I lock eyes with the beautiful woman sitting front and center.

"Mabel? Like everything I do, this is for you."

Then, for the first time in over fifteen years, I summon the Poison Puppetmaster heavy metal voice of my youth, and I sing.

MABEL MCGONIGLE, YOU ARE MY FAVORITE GIRL
WHEN YOU SMILE, YOU LIGHT UP THE WHOLE WORLD

I LOVE YOU!
I LOVE YOU!
I LOVE YOU SO MUCH!
YOU ARE THE GIRL THAT I LOVE TO TOUCH!

I WANT TO SEE THE WORLD WITH YOU BY MY SIDE
WILL YOU MAKE ME SO HAPPY BY BEING MY BRIDE?

With that, I get down on one knee and pull out the ring I've been dying to give her since we boarded our flight.

Mabel rushes onstage with tears in her eyes and tackles me.

"Ooof!" We hit the ground. She kisses me until we're both breathless and almost roll off the stage.

I pull her up to stand with me center stage. "Is that a yes?"

She beams at me and cups my cheeks in her hands. "Do honeybees see blue better than red?"

I chuckle. "I have absolutely no idea."

"They do! Yes, yes, yes, I'll marry you!"

I slip the ring on her finger and dip her back into another deep kiss.

The family band crescendos.

The audience applauds on their feet.

And all feels right in the world.

Because I'm about to marry the girl of my dreams.

Epilogue

MABEL

"This brings new meaning to 'Wally and Mabel sitting in a tree.'" Wally pulls me close and nuzzles my neck.

I happily wrap my arm across his muscular chest. "Do you like it?"

"I love it."

It's one of those lazy end-of-summer nights with the perfect amount of breeze, and the right temperature. We're sprawled out high up in the huge double hammock I just had installed in my favorite corner of our tree farm. It stretches between these four big old Maple trees—or *Mabel* trees as Wally likes to call them— where we love to picnic in the daytime and watch fireflies at night.

"I thought our firefly watch point deserved an upgrade. I also wanted to do something special to thank you for spending all that time with me in the Netherlands. I know extending our trip two weeks was a lot to ask."

"Mabey Baby." He kisses the top of my head. "After all you've given me? You could ask for the whole world, and that still wouldn't be asking enough."

I silently respond by snuggling closer.

"And I'm glad we stayed as long as we did," Wally continues. "It was great getting to know your new family slowly and under less... dramatic circumstances."

"There's only so much you can learn about people while proposing and performing folksy family-friendly music together, right?" I laugh.

"Exactly. Though, I'd venture to say they learned a little too much about *us* that first night onstage. Our style was less family friendly and a bit more in your face."

I startle and prop myself on an elbow. "Did you just ask me to *sit more on your face*?"

Wally bursts out laughing and props himself up too. "Talk about perfectly illustrating my point! No, I did not say that. But— you know what? What the hell? Think this hammock can handle our sorts of shenanigans? If we fall to our deaths, at least we die happy, right?" He lies back again and smacks his chest. "Lay it on me, baby."

"Stop." I shove him playfully, then yank his shirt to pull him up to sitting. "Sorry, my head's a bit all over the place right now. Guess I'm hearing things."

"Maybe we're just at the point in our relationship where you're reading my mind," he suggests with a silly waggle of his eyebrows.

"Maybe." I stare out toward the grove of "Mabel trees" Wally planted last year. It's amazing seeing how much they've grown.

Time goes by so fast sometimes.

I want to gobble up every second.

"What's up?" He softens his voice and runs a hand down my back.

A firefly lands on the hammock. Her light blinks over and over, almost like she's saying "Ask him. Ask him. Ask him."

I take a deep breath. "Remember a moment ago when you said that super romantic thing about how after everything I've given you, I could ask for the world and it still wouldn't be asking enough?"

"Yes..."

"Well brace yourself big guy, because I'm about to ask for something pretty big."

"Consider me braced..."

"I know we said we wanted to get married here on our farm, something simple and small, and I still love that idea..."

"But?" He runs his fingers through my hair.

"*But*... after everything we just experienced overseas, I want to experience the world as much as I can, and there are so many places I've never been and—"

"Where are we going, fiancée?" He caresses my cheek.

I love when he calls me that.

"Really? You're open to a new plan?"

"Absolutely, as long as the result is still marrying you."

"Oh it is! I want to marry the shit out of you. In Hawaii. At James and Louise's place."

"Whoa," Wally breathes. "I'm into the idea, but they're about to have a baby. Should they really be hosting a wedding?"

"Louise says she needs the distraction." I shrug, then let the excitement overtake me. "We spent our whole Entreprewhore session this afternoon planning it out. Okay, so here's the plan. We'll get married in two weeks on the beach. We looped James into our brainstorm—he's going to call you later tonight with all sorts of info—and he's being awesome as always. And so resourceful! With The Highs and Lows, he's used to helping people get to Hawaii, right? So anyway, he has *all* the contacts. He's already got us a great group rate at the resort he partners with, so people will have a place to stay. He and Louise know a great company they say can provide some simple, delicious catering. Oh! And he even found reasonable flights for everyone! So now all we have to do is reach out to our family and friends and see if they can make it and—"

"Sorry to interrupt—did you just say two weeks?"

I wince. "Yeah?"

"We're getting married in *two weeks*?"

"If that's okay with you?"

"You're telling me that in two weeks, I get to officially start the rest of my life with the most beautiful, kind, and hilarious woman I've ever met? I get to love her and cherish her for better or worse; for richer or poorer; in sickness and in health till death do us part?"

"That's what I'm telling you!" I clap my hands, press him back on the hammock and cover him with kisses. He wraps his strong arms around me and holds me tight.

After a few moments, Wally's hold loosens, and I roll onto my back beside him. We lie there, fingers intertwined, watching the fireflies overhead, and I can't help but wonder how I ever got this lucky.

"Whatcha thinking?" he whispers and squeezes my hand.

I tip my gaze up to look at him. "About how happy I am, and also how gloomy those traditional vows are. Poverty? Sickness? Death? No thank you. The vows I'm writing for us are way better."

"You already wrote us wedding vows?" he asks.

I tap my temple. "They're forming right now. As we speak."

"Oh boy," he laughs.

"And wait till you hear them, buddy. They're a doozy."

Wally laughs and pulls me closer, bringing my head to rest over his heart.

He lets out a happy sigh. "From you, Mabey Baby? I wouldn't expect anything less."

Baitin'

Chapter One

LOUISE

"It's official. I'm a priest!" James announces as he swoops into the kitchen and plants a kiss on my cheek.

"Whoa!" Calliope exclaims from my phone.

I'm sitting at our breakfast bar eating a bowl of fruit and yogurt while chatting with Mabel and Calliope on our weekly support call.

"Oh! Hello, Rich Bitches!" James leans in front of the screen for a second and grabs an apple from the counter.

"Hi, James." Mabel waves. "Hey, ladies? I still don't think that's the most accurate title for our group. I mean, are any of us actually rich?"

"Not yet," Calliope says. "But we're working on it! And you gotta believe to receive, right?"

Calliope has turned over a new leaf when it comes to her author business and general outlook on life. A few months ago, she was all fear and anxiety. These days, she's choosing gratitude and calmness and flow.

It's a good look on her.

I could use some of that positive energy myself.

Because I'm thirty-seven weeks pregnant today, and I don't think I'm doing so well with the whole experience. Am I grateful this baby is on the way? Absolutely. Am I calm about his or her impending arrival? Hell no.

Which is probably why I offered to host twenty-five humans for a surprise last-minute beach wedding on our property in less than a week. In hindsight, I can see how maybe that wasn't the wisest decision to make this close to my due date, but I'm telling myself it will all be fine. James and I love Mabel and Wally to the moon and back, so we're happy to offer them this kind of support, and after two successful years running our excursion company – The Highs and Lows – we know we're an awesome team when it comes to showing groups of people a good time. Selfishly, what feels most important right now is that becoming their impromptu wedding planner has given my brain exactly what it needs: something to focus on other than becoming a mother.

"You gotta believe to receive," Mabel repeats. "I like that! Where did you hear it?"

Calliope waves her off. "Oh, some self-help crap I'm reading. It's embarrassing to talk about, but hot damn, this shit works! Anyway, can we circle back to James's announcement? He's a *priest* now?"

"He meant that he completed his online minister certification," I explain between bites of cantaloupe.

"Eh," Calliope grunts. "Becoming a priest would have been way sexier."

"Excuse me?" James and I say at the same time. He pulls up a stool beside me and kisses my shoulder.

I don't mean to, but I pull away slightly.

I smile and pretend it didn't happen.

He pretends not to notice.

This is our new, sad dance.

"Oh yeah," Calliope says. "Priests are basically a taboo romance subgenre now. They take forbidden relationships to a whole other level. Because in these stories, it's not just warring families or the threat of a lost inheritance trying to keep the lovers apart, it's God! The stakes couldn't be higher." She pauses. "Damn! Why haven't I written a dinosaur priest love story yet?"

"Get on it, girl!" Mabel claps. "Oh my gosh, a Brontosaurus with its super long neck would be so cute on the cover wearing the priesty neck collar thingy, don't you think?!"

"I *do* think, Mabes, I do!" Calliope's eyes twinkle with excitement. "Important question, though. Would the priesty neck collar thingy be at the top of his long neck or at the bottom?"

"Top," James says at the same moment that I say, "Bottom."

Just one more silly disagreement in a long line of them lately.

"You're right," Calliope says. "It's negotiable. Maybe I'll ask my designer to try placing it in the middle."

"Can I get you some of your tea?" James asks me softly, wonderful as always.

"That would be good, thanks."

He kisses me on the head, then crosses to the stove and fills the kettle with water.

Calliope lets out an uncharacteristic squeal. "Eeeee! The magic of ideas! Do you guys mind if I bail from the call a few minutes early so I can hit the ground running with this one? I feel like everything flows better if I start plotting as soon as the idea lands."

"Sure!" I say. "Go with God! Or, in the case of this Brontosaurus priest, go... *against* God?"

Her eyes gleam. "Oh, I will!" She grabs a notebook and clutches it to her chest. "I'll see you in three days, friends! Mabes, get ready for the bachelorette party of the century, baby!"

"I'm ready, assholes!" Mabel punches the air in delight, then backtracks when we both look at her in confusion. "'Assholes sounded mean, huh? I always call you bitches *bitches,* so I thought I'd shake things up this one time and try calling you assholes." She shrugs. "Didn't work. No biggie. Okay, happy writing, Callie! And safe flight this weekend! Love you!"

Calliope beams. "Love you too! Both of you!" She logs off, leaving me alone with Mabel.

Wow. Calliope is letting go of her angst. Mabel is getting married. I'm about to have a baby. A lot is changing in our little group.

"Is James still there?" Mabel squints at her screen.

"Yeah, he's just —"

"Yes, Mrs. Bieber? You rang?"

James sock slides up beside me, but noticeably doesn't touch me this time. And dammit, now I wish he would. What is going on with me?

"Ooooooooh." Mabel shudders. "Mrs. Bieber. That sounds fun. But I don't think we're going that route. Nice sock slide, by the way."

"I thank you," James says. "No Mrs. Bieber, huh? Should I start addressing my friend as Wallace McGonigle?"

"Nah. I think we're going to do a combo name situation

instead. Like Mr. and Mrs. McBieber. Or The Biebonigles."

I snort laugh. "The Biebonigles! That's amazing!" I pause when I see the blank expression on Mabel's face. "Oh, you're serious."

"Completely." A smile spreads across her face. "How cool would it be if someday Wally and I have a whole litter of Biebonigles?" She hesitates. "Hm. *Litter* sounds kinda derogatory, though, doesn't it? Gosh, poor puppies, am I right? They deserve a better group name than something that sounds like trash."

"You know who has it good on that front?" James says. "Birds. A gaggle of geese. A parliament of owls. A *kettle* of hawks." He points at the perfectly timed squeal of our kettle, then gets up to assemble my tea. "Oh, and my favorite... a *flamboyance* of flamingoes. How fun is that?"

"How do you know so much about bird groupings?" I shout toward the kitchen.

He shrugs. "All those years of travel. You'd be surprised how many birdwatchers you meet. People love their birdwatching."

"Bugs have some good groupings too!" Mabel says. "An army of caterpillars. A cloud of grasshoppers. A pledge of wasps. How about marine animals, Lou?"

I'm not sure we're going down this pointless road when there are lots of wedding details to discuss, but Mabel is always good for taking us on fun tangents. And right now, tangents are kind of my thing.

"Sure, there are fun ones in the water. A shiver of sharks..."

Mabel shudders. "A shiver of sharks. Oooooooh."

"A smack of jellyfish. A fever of stingrays. A bloat of hippopotami." I hesitate. "But hippopotami technically aren't considered marine animals. They're semi-aquatic. Though recent studies are showing they are close evolutionary relatives of whales and dolphins, so whatever, let's count them."

James places my tea down in front of me.

"Thanks, babe."

Mabel changes topics. "How are you feeling, Louise? How grows that bay-bay in your va-jay-jay?"

I consider stating the obvious. That the bay-bay is not technically in my va-jay-jay. But Mabel is just being cute and doesn't need to be corrected. She's a grown woman who knows how the human body works. But at this point, it really is just semantics because in approximately three weeks, the bay-bay *will* be in my va-jay-jay, stretching and ripping and tearing and…

"Your face just went white," James says. "You okay?"

I snap out of my scary visualization, ignore Mabel's well-meaning question, and say, "Yup! Hey, you missed a few good bird groups, ya know."

James tilts his head to the side. "Did I now?"

"Sure did! A bouquet of pheasants. A lamentation of swans. A pandemonium of parrots. I mean, how fun is that one? But there are some really great ones outside of birds, bugs, and marine animals too. A conspiracy of lemurs. A wisdom of wombats. A prickle of porcupines? Come on! That one has to be my favorite."

"Louise's *Jeopardy* obsession strikes again!" Mabel says. "This is why you always want this girl on your trivia team."

"True, true," James says, but he's looking at me with concern. Because he knows when the *Jeopardy* stuff rears its head, that means I'm getting swallowed up by anxiety. "Hey, Mabes?" he asks. "Is it cool if we sign off now? Louise and I have some things we need to talk about."

"No, we don't," I say.

"Yes," he says firmly. "We do."

Mabel's eyes dart back and forth between the two of us. "Absolutely. Go, go, go! We'll see you at the airport tomorrow, Jamesy! And listen, if I haven't said it enough today, thank you both so much for this. I hope helping us with the wedding so close to the baby being born isn't causing tension between you two."

"Nope! No tension!" I say, the now obvious tension rolling off me in waves.

James smiles and says softly, "No tension, Mabel. No worries."

She smiles wide, but her eyes still look worried. "Okay. Mrs. Mabel Biebonigle is signing off!"

With that, her image disappears, and James and I are left alone at the breakfast bar.

I focus on sipping my tea, but I can feel him staring at me.

"Are we okay?" he asks.

"Of course, we're okay. Why would you ask that?" I slurp my tea way louder and longer than necessary.

"You just seem really... off."

I laugh. "Off? You think I'm off? What are you talking about? I am *on*. I am soooo on. I'm running painting workshops on the beach five mornings a week while helping you run a full-time water excursion company. I'm cooking a baby, stepmomming the heck out of Iris, *and* throwing our best friends a beautiful beach wedding all at the same time. I ask you, who is *on*-er than me?"

"All excellent points." He smiles, then sighs. "Join me on the couch, will you?"

"Sure! I love the couch!"

I follow him to the living room and sit beside him. Well, not exactly *beside* him. I make sure there is a couch cushion of space between us.

James looks at the empty cushion, then into my eyes. "Can we agree that maybe you've taken on a little too much?"

"Pfffft." I look out the window toward the ocean. "I can handle 'too much.'"

"Just because you *can* doesn't mean you have to," he says. "Say the word, and whatever you need taken off your plate, I'm your guy. You hear me, Lou? I'll shoulder whatever you can't carry right now. I mean, you're carrying our baby, right? It's the least I can do."

I keep my eyes on the ocean as they start to water. Other than a sniffle, I stay silent.

"Can I tell you the other reason I asked if we're okay?"

I shrug. "Sure."

"Every time I touch you lately, you flinch."

"That's not true."

He closes the distance between us and places his hand on my belly.

I flinch. "I'M SORRY, BUT HOW MANY PENISES CAN I HAVE INSIDE ME AT ONCE?!"

He immediately lifts his hand and shoots to his feet. "Excuse me? What?"

I'm embarrassed by my outburst, but I try to save face and say, "You heard me."

"I *heard* you, yeah, but how the hell am I supposed to answer that?" He searches for some viable responses. "As many as you put your mind to? One? I hope? Preferably mine?" He pauses. "Louise. Seriously. What are you talking about?"

I cover my face with a throw pillow. "Can I have a hug?"

My words are muffled, but he hears me. He always hears me.

"Of course you can. Come here."

He tosses the pillow to the side and pulls me up to stand. I sink right into his arms. Actually, it's probably more effective to say I *tip* into his arms. My belly is so big now that any time I try to hug someone, it involves tipping my chest forward and sticking my butt way back. It's awkward. But so is sleeping, peeing, standing and shoe-tying. It all feels incredibly awkward.

"It feels so good to hold you, Cold Brew," he murmurs into my hair.

"Oh my God." I chuckle. "I thought we retired that nickname."

"I like to bring it out of the vault occasionally. To remind you that once upon a time you were super into me."

"Once upon a time?" I pull back slightly so I can look at him. "James. I'm still super into you. I love you."

"I love you too. More than anything. Which is why I'm worried about you." He strokes my hair. "Talk to me, will you? And please explain your multiple penis outburst as soon as possible because my brain is coming up with all kinds of disturbing scenarios around that one."

I take a deep breath and launch in. "I'm freaking out, James. I thought this was all supposed to feel natural, but it doesn't. I mean, I'm happy we're doing this." I rub my hands over my belly. "I'm *so* happy we're doing this, but... I'm scared."

He tilts his head to the side. "Of being a mom? You're already an amazing bonus mom to Iris."

"I know." I sigh. "I mean, thanks. But Iris is easy. My role with her is easy. I came into her life after she was already a walking, talking amazing little kid with two awesome parents she depends on. I could basically just be her friend. Also, she didn't camp out in my uterus, stomp on my bladder, and give me constant terrifying reminders that she plans on tearing up my undercarriage any day now."

"Your undercarriage?" James chuckles.

"Mabel suggested we all watch *Bridesmaids* before next weekend to 'get hyped' for the wedding. I watched it while you were on a tour yesterday. I love that scene when Melissa McCarthy harasses Airline Marshall Jon on the plane."

"Who doesn't?" He gently backs me up against the window and puts his foot on the windowsill so he's half-straddling me. "You feel that heat? That's coming from my undercarriage."

I laugh. "Excellent Melissa McCarthy impression."

"I thought you'd like it."

For a moment, that old feeling between us comes back. That magnetic pull that usually won't let us keep our hands off each other. He places his foot back on the floor and slides his hands up my neck and into my hair. We kiss, deep and slow. It feels so good. It's been too long. It's such a relief and...

"The multiple penis thing!" I shout.

He stops kissing me and pulls back, dazed. "Hm?"

I continue in a quieter tone, "You, um... You asked me to explain the multiple penis thing and why I've been so flinchy and hands-off lately."

He smiles and says, "Proceed," but he's clearly not ready to stop touching me. While I talk, he peppers soft kisses down my neck.

"I had this thought last month when we were having sex – and yes, I realize it's been a whole month, and I miss it and *you*, but –"

He continues to rain kisses down my body, letting his lips brush over my collarbones, my breasts...

My voice goes breathy. "Anyway, here's the thought. If the baby is a boy, then there is a penis inside me twenty-four seven. So when yours got... *involved* that night, I realized there were potentially two penises inside me simultaneously. And they were related to each other. The whole concept creeped me out."

"My penis creeped you out?"

"No. Just like... the *thought* of it."

"Oh, well that's better!" He laughs, but I can tell I'm hurting his feelings.

He's down on his knees now, where he was about to kiss my belly. He gives up on that and tentatively wraps his arms around my waist instead. I run my hands over his buzz-cut hair, a tingly feeling on my palms that I've always loved.

"It's not just the sex thing," I say. "It's… It's like I don't recognize this body I'm living in. It's weird giving up control, you know? Every day there's a new symptom, a new restriction. I mean, geezuz have you seen what my boobs are up to lately?"

"Oh, I've seen 'em." He looks up at me and winks.

"They're bigger than my head and twice as heavy."

He smiles. "Like I said, I am here to shoulder the extra weight, lady."

James places his hands under my enormous breasts and gives them a lift. And dammit if it doesn't feel like sweet relief. The lifting of the physical weight, but the emotional weight too. It feels so good to laugh with him again and tell him how I've really been feeling.

I playfully swat his hands away. "Alright, you dirty dog."

"Woof!" he jokes.

I attempt a wide-legged squat and offer him my hands. "Here. Help me down."

"What, you want to get down on the floor with me?"

"I do," I say mid-squat. "So help me, please. This sort of thing isn't as easy as it was eight-and-a-half months ago."

He guides me down until we sit on the hardwood floor, facing each other. I butt scooch as close to James as my belly will allow and wrap my legs around him. He weaves his fingers together behind me, creating a backrest for me.

I place my forehead against his and just breathe with him for a moment. "You know who else is pregnant?"

"Who?" he asks softly.

"Meilani. The team in Monterey sent me a message today."

"No way! Is this good news?"

"Seems to be. They say she's in great spirits and will give birth any day now."

"Wow." James kneads his knuckles up and down the muscles surrounding my spine, just the way I like. It feels like heaven.

"I wish they'd told me sooner. Maybe we could have taken another trip up to see her."

Meilani is the incredible California sea lion I bonded with during my time on staff at the Philadelphia Aquarium. She taught me so much in such a short time. About resilience. About unconditional love. She was even the catalyst for getting me back in touch with my artistic sensibilities. When I look at my life now and how wonderful it is, I feel like I can trace so much of it back to her. I wish I could be there for her now the way she was there for me.

Soon after the aquarium moved Meilani back to Monterey and I relocated to Hawaii, we had a nice flow of communication going. James, Iris, and I took a great family trip up to California to see her in her new digs and meet her team in person. After that, the team sent me videos every few weeks. And every month or so, we would do a video call so she and I could connect in real time. Occasionally they even set her up with her canvases and brushes so we could paint together, just like old times.

But everything shifts over time, right?

Staff shake-ups at the marine center and lots of life changes for me meant our communication gradually started slipping through the cracks.

I miss her.

"They have a birth cam set up by her tank," I say. "So I can tune in whenever I want."

"Are you going to do that?" He continues massaging up and down my back.

"I don't know. Maybe. I understand that it's science, and everyone at the center is excited, but it feels like an invasion of her privacy, you know? Like that would be my absolute worst nightmare, having a whole audience assembled and watching me give birth." I shake my head. "No way. Just you, me, and the doctor. That's it."

"Oh, am I invited? The jury was out for a while on whether I was allowed in the room."

"I was never serious about that." I give him a gentle shove.

He laughs. "You sure about that? Because you seemed pretty serious."

I sigh and look him deep in the eyes. "You are amazing. And you're doing everything right for me. I'm sorry I've been so..."

"Beautiful? Insightful?" He fills in my blanks.

"You think I'm beautiful right now?" I snort.

"Louise? I've never been more attracted to you than I am at this moment. And this is coming from the guy who wanted you so badly the second he saw you that he had to instantly drag you into a walk-in refrigerator and have his way with you."

My cheeks heat. "That's very sweet, but if memory serves, *I* was the one who had to drag *you* into that refrigerator."

"You remember it your way. I remember it mine." He places a warm hand on my face and plants a soft kiss on my lips.

"Insightful, though?" My eyebrows scrunch together. "How am I being insightful right now?"

"You're... in tune. With how you're feeling. Listen, I've never carried a baby myself, but from what I've seen and understand, it can be a bit of an emotional roller coaster. It's not always pink and blue fluffy cuteness like the movies make you believe." He places his hands on my belly. "There's some primal shit happening in here."

"Primal shit, huh?"

"Yeah. Your body is a sexy baby jungle right now, and I'm here for it."

"Oh my God, stop talking." I laugh and shove him.

"Come here."

He holds me and strokes my hair.

The sound of ocean waves wafts through the window.

"Can I say one more thing, though?" he says softly. "In all seriousness."

"I guess?"

"It's okay not to love every second of this. Maybe it would help to talk to someone who's been through it and can understand where you're at."

"Yeah, maybe." I sigh, having no idea who that person would be. My mom is out of the question, and I'm the first of my friends to go down this path. "If only Meilani could talk, right?"

He kisses me on the forehead. "You're doing great, Lou. This is the home stretch. We'll take it one day at a time."

I close my eyes and rest my head on his shoulder. "One day at a time."

Chapter Two

JAMES

I'm standing on the curb outside of the arrivals entrance holding a sign that says, "Welcome to Hawaii, Mr. & Mrs. Biebonigle!" when a telltale squeal reverberates inside the revolving doors, signaling that the spirited bride-to-be has, in fact, arrived.

"Jamesy!" Mabel bursts onto the sidewalk and straddle jumps me. I drop the sign just in time to catch her – I am a gentleman, after all – but I quickly look at Wally for his take on the situation.

"It's fine." He shrugs as he approaches. "Straddle-jump greetings are sort of her thing."

Mabel hops down and nods vigorously. "They really are."

"Fun!" I say as I pick up the sign and reach to take a bag from Wally. "This probably goes without saying, Mabes, but I'd recommend *not* using the straddle-jump approach with Louise right now."

"Oh, of course not! Baby on board! Honk, honk!" She honks an imaginary celebratory car horn in the air. "Gosh, Jamesy, thank you for everything you're doing. I'm so excited you're marrying us. I mean officiating the ceremony. Whew! For a second there, it sounded like I was inviting you to join Wally and me as a throuple!"

Mabel is the greatest. I'm so happy she came into my buddy's life. And into mine too. She's become the weirdo little sister I never had.

"Listen." I place an arm around each of them. "I love both of you Biebonigles..."

"Oooooh. The name is totally catching on!" Mabel pops Wally in the gut.

"But your fiancé is way too grumpy in the mornings for me to even consider throupling with you. Besides, I am completely committed to and enthralled by my beautiful baby mama."

"How's Louise feeling today?" Wally asks.

"Good. She's good. She's sorry she couldn't be here to pick you guys up with me. She has a private painting session this morning."

"Oh my gosh, completely understandable," Mabel says. "I feel a little funny about this whole thing, actually. It's my understanding that most human women want to relax and do nothing this close to giving birth, not help host a wedding."

"Well, Louise isn't most human women."

"I agree! She's not. She's more like the tsetse fly! Entomologists call the tsetse fly the 'supermom of the insect world' because they just go about their regular fly lives, getting pregnant every ten days and birthing baby bugs that are their size or larger. They're total ballers. Just like Louise."

I tilt my head to the side. "Interesting assessment, Mabes. The baby is measuring on the larger side, and I agree that Louise is awesome, but maybe we should hold off on comparing her to blood-sucking insects for now?"

"You're right, you're right. It's easy for me to forget that not everyone sees bugs as the magical beautiful creatures that I do. Ix-nay on the ugs-bay."

"Alright. Why are we standing here, party people? My car is right over here."

We roll their luggage toward my car.

"How was the flight, friends?" I ask.

"Productive," Wally says. "I finally finished writing my vows."

"You didn't tell me that!" Mabel says and smacks him on the butt.

"You were unconscious and snoring most of the flight, madam. Hard to tell you anything."

Mabel laughs and opens the rear door of my hatchback when we reach it. Wally and I start tossing the bags inside.

"Isn't this the part where most women insist they don't snore?" I ask.

"That would be pointless," she says. "I know who I am. I snore like a beast when I'm upright. But lay me on my belly or my side, and I'm a quiet delight."

Wally goes all googly-eyed at his fiancée and presses her into my car. "Quiet or loud, on your back or your belly, you, my lady, are sweet as apple-honey jelly."

"Aw, Walla-Walla," Mabel coos.

They proceed to make out aggressively against my bumper.

This goes on for a minute.

I look at my watch.

I'm all for public displays of affection, but these two are something else sometimes.

I'm about to pour a proverbial bucket of water on them when a powder-blue van pulls up behind us and does it for me. A series of beeps ring out. A horrified mother steps out of the driver's seat and glares at my soon-to-be-married friends while she lets not one, not two, but five young children out of the vehicle. They all step onto the sidewalk and stare at the sensual scene unfolding against my car.

"Guys?" I tap Wally on the shoulder. "Maybe we can wrap this up and save it for the wedding night? Or at least until you're in a room with four walls and no observant children?"

They untangle themselves and take in the family assembled on the sidewalk. "Aloha, everyone!" Mabel waves and says to the mother, "Hard to keep our hands off each other. We're getting married this weekend!"

"Congratulations," the woman huffs and ushers her children through the revolving door.

"Shall we?" I smile and open the front passenger side for Mabel.

"Fuck a duck on a stick! My buglorette bag!" She freezes and places her hands over her mouth.

I look at Wally. "Did any of that make sense to you?"

"I checked my buglorette bag with all my bachelorette goodies and forgot to grab it off the belt. Oh my God, we need to get it!"

"No problem, Mabey Baby," Wally says. "Why don't you chill in the car, and James and I will see about your bag?"

"Bless you, Bing Bang." She gives him a quick kiss and hops

in the car.

I give Wally a confused look as we walk back toward the building.

"Bing Bang is short for Walla-Walla Bing Bang," he says sheepishly.

"Ah." I sigh. "You guys are doing really great, huh?"

"Thanks for sounding so happy about that, friend," Wally says sarcastically.

"No, I *am* happy for you. Of course, I am. I'm just... I'm a little worried for me. For us. Me and Louise, I mean."

"What's going on?"

"She's just really out of sorts. She seems so stressed and worried about the birth and everything that comes after it. And... I have no idea how to make it all okay for her."

"Give yourself more credit. This isn't your first rodeo, pal." He slaps me on the back and pushes me through the door. "You've done this before."

I shake my head as travelers hustle all around us. "Totally different. When Eva was pregnant with Iris, we were two good friends making the best out of a tricky situation. The stakes were high, of course, and I did whatever I could to support the hell out of her, but it didn't feel like this." I sigh. "Lou is the love of my life, man. There's not a second of the day when she's not on my mind. I want to be the man who gives her what she needs. The guy who makes her feel safe and adored. I want her to know in the deepest parts of her heart that we are unstoppable together. That no matter what comes our way, with her hand in mine, we'll make it through and be better than before. Life is an unpredictable epic journey. There will always be twists and turns and storms to weather. But if we do it together, we will be like the rainbow soaring across the sky after the hurricane, our colors blending and swirling to create something beautiful and powerful and true."

Wally stops walking and looks me square in the face.

"Dude, what the fuck?"

My brow furrows. "What? Was that weird?"

"Hell yeah, it was weird! Really weird, dude." He looks left and right, like he's embarrassed to be seen with me.

"Oh! Sure." I throw my hands up. "This from the guy who proposed marriage via rhyming monster rap."

"It was not a *rap*. It was a heavy metal improvisational declaration of love."

"Right," I scoff. "Totally normal."

"Fine. We're both cornball idiots for the women we love," Wally admits. He hesitates. "Can I say something?"

"Why not? Don't spare my feelings now, *Bing Bang*."

The moment that nickname comes out of my mouth, I know I will never be saying it again. Wally gives me a look that makes it clear he feels the same way.

"I'll stick to calling you Wally from now on," I say.

"Good man." He spots a bench nearby and leads me to it. "Here. Sit for a second, will ya?"

I land heavily on the seat and scrub my hands over my face. "Lay it on me. Whatcha got?"

"All ribbing aside? You said something just now that concerned me. You said, 'I have no idea how to make it all okay for her.' What makes you think that's your job?"

I look at him, but I don't have an immediate response.

"That's not something we can do for people. Not even the people we love most. I couldn't make it all okay for Mabel when we'd just met, and her family was falling apart. You couldn't make it all okay for me a few years ago when I got sick. But look at Mabel and me now. She wrestled with her shit. I wrestled with mine. And now here we are, together, better than ever – how did you phrase it? – blending and swirling like a fucking love rainbow?"

I laugh. "Those weren't my *exact* words, but... point taken."

"Be there for Louise. Keep letting her know you're there for her every step of the way. Just keep in mind that some things she may need to wrestle with on her own." He pauses. "You know, I've been thinking..." He stops himself again. "No, never mind. Probably not my place."

"What's not your place? Being all up in my business?" I laugh. "You're ass-deep in my business, so why pull yourself out now?"

He smiles. "Alright. Feel free to tell me I'm full of shit because I'm certainly no therapist, but... is it possible Louise has some family issues she still needs to work out? I mean, did she ever *really* deal with all that stuff she had going on with her parents?"

"Sort of?" I say. "A little?"

Wally shrugs and tries to act like he's not detonating truth bombs with every word he says. "It just seems to me that when you're becoming a parent yourself, it might bring up feelings about your own parental figures. And if that relationship is complicated, it might cause some complicated feelings."

"Damn, Bieber!" I say, impressed.

He shrugs again.

"You know, with all this sound advice you're dispensing, you're gonna make a pretty great parent yourself one day."

"Well. Mabel did repeatedly beg me to 'pollinate' her onstage in the Netherlands." He smiles proudly. "But we've decided to hold off a few years on kids. We're happy being Aunt Mabel and Uncle Wally to your kids for now." He slaps a hand on my shoulder. "Listen. However we can help, we're always here for you guys, okay?"

"Thanks, man." My phone rings in my pocket. "Damn, I forgot I have a call with the caterer about something."

"Take it. I have a buglorette bag to rescue."

He hoists himself off the bench and walks through the bustling tourists toward baggage claim.

"Hey!" I call out to him. "Please tell me your wedding vows don't rhyme. And there won't be improvisational singing during the ceremony?"

"It's our day, punk!" he shouts over his shoulder. "We'll do what we want."

Wally disappears down the escalator. And not for the first or even the hundredth time, I thank my lucky stars I have that grumpy jerk in my life.

I pick up the phone without looking at the screen. "James here. Thanks for your email about the appetizer situation."

"Appetizer situation?" a female voice says.

"I'm sorry, I thought this was the – Sorry, who's calling?"

"Oh, this couldn't have worked out any better! I got your number off The Highs and Lows website because I wanted to surprise her – I'm not sure why I didn't have it before – and then I came up the escalator and saw you sitting there with a man who looks like Thor and everything felt like it was falling into place, so I dialed your number and –"

"I'm sorry, ma'am, could you slow down, please? I'm not sure what's going on and –"

"Look to your right," she says.

I do, and what I see makes my mouth drop open.

"You didn't think I would miss the birth of this beautiful baby, did you?" she says, a giddy smile on her face.

Oh man. Let the family healing begin.

Chapter Three

LOUISE

"Coming!" I shout as I waddle my way to answer the doorbell.

Shit. I'm officially waddling. I thought the pregnancy waddle was a myth, but apparently not. As of this morning, it is a personal reality.

I consciously lengthen my strides and look through the peephole. A beautiful woman with jet-black silken hair waits on the stoop with a sleeping baby strapped to her chest and my eight-year-old best buddy standing beside her.

I swing the door open, and Iris runs straight into my arms. "Mamalou!"

She started calling me Mamalou about a year into my relationship with James. It's adorable and I love it, but sometimes I wonder if I should ask Eva if she minds.

"Eva." I give her a quick hug after Iris lets me go. "How many times have I told you? You don't have to ring the bell. This is Iris's house too. And you're always welcome. Just come right inside. Always!"

"I know, I know," she says in a hushed voice.

"Oh sorry." I lower my voice and peek into the baby carrier. "Is she sleeping?"

"Yeah," Eva says. "This wrap is like baby crack. We'd barely taken two steps outside, and she nodded right off. They say it reminds them of being back in the womb. Do you have one yet? I have to get you one."

"You've already given us so much," I protest.

"Well get ready, lady, because I'm about to give you more."

She hands me a paper shopping bag filled with onesies and

baby footie pajamas.

"Wow," I say as I rummage around inside. "Thank you. Here. Come in, come in."

I hold the door open wide for them as they step inside and slip their shoes off.

"No, thank *you*. People don't tell you this before you become a parent, but hand-me-downs help the giver way more than the receiver. It's like 'Please! Get this stuff out of my house!'" she laughs. "Anyway" – she kisses her baby on the head – "this li'l bugger is moving into six-to-nine-month clothes, so –"

"So whatever doesn't fit anymore is for Buttmunch." Iris finishes her mother's sentence for her.

"Rissy," Eva gently scolds. "I told you, we're not going to do that." She turns to me. "I'm sorry. She's been calling your baby Buttmunch."

I know Eva is trying to have a serious parenting moment, but I can't help my laughter. "Buttmunch? Really, Riss? Why are you calling the baby Buttmunch?"

"Because all my friends at school have fun nicknames for their brothers and sisters. Krystal calls her sister Pom-Pom Butt. Jeremiah's twin brother and sister are Butt One and Butt Two. And Tommy calls his baby brother the Mayor of Butt Town."

"Do all the nicknames involve the word 'butt'?" I ask.

Eva nods. "They do."

"Third grade sounds awesome so far, huh?" I ruffle my buddy's hair.

"It really is," Iris says with seriousness.

I place the bag of newly acquired clothes in what has quickly become "baby corner," a section of our living room where we've been putting the lovely gifts that keep arriving from friends and family. There's a Diaper Genie from my old team at the Philadelphia Aquarium, a baby bathtub, and tons of little bath toys from Ralph and Calliope. And a big box from my mother that arrived months ago and remains unopened.

Eva gives me a confused look.

"I know it's a bit of a mess. We're almost done with the nursery. I just haven't finished the wall mural I want to do yet, so we're keeping the stuff out here for now."

She nods and smiles.

"Okay." I rub my hands together and look at Iris. "Are we ready to paint?"

"Let's doooooooo it!" she squeals.

"Lead the way, girly," I say and watch her tear to the sliding screen door leading out to the beach, where I already have our easels and materials all set up.

Around the time that Eva and her husband Ron announced they were having a baby, I decided to host this monthly paint party for Iris, her mom, and me. Just the three of us girls. From the moment I met James's daughter, I knew she was special. And I count myself lucky every day that I get to be a part of her life. This felt like a small, fun thing I could do to get to know her mom better and make sure she grows up knowing that all her parental figures love her and put her first.

Eva grabs my hand and swings it as we follow Iris onto the sand. "You sure you're doing okay?"

"Yeah, I'm fine," I say, but I'm not sure how convincing I am.

"Because if you ever want to run any this birth and baby stuff by me – and I understand if that's too weird for you and you'd rather not – I'm here for you."

"Thank you. That's really nice."

I've always liked Eva – she's virtually impossible *not* to like – but somewhere along the line, she became a friend, not just my boyfriend's daughter's mother. I think about what James said last night about finding someone to talk to who's been through this whole experience. I look down at my belly, then at our connected hands and feel silly that I didn't even consider confiding in her until now. Because surprisingly, it's not weird at all.

I start with something small. "I've been getting more of those Braxton Hicks contraction thingies, but that's normal, right?"

She nods. "Totally normal, yeah."

"We're painting starfishes today?!" Iris squeals as she reaches our easels and sees the assortment of dried starfish I've laid out for us.

"We are!" I smile. "I thought it would be a good choice since you said you're learning about starfish in science class this week."

"Look, Mom!" Iris holds up a starfish and points at various

parts. "These are the limbs. This is its mouth. And did you know that at the end of each arm is a microscopic eye that can detect whether it's light or dark outside?"

"Is that true?" Eva looks at me.

I nod. "True indeed."

I love that Iris shares my love of sea creatures.

"Shall we?" I gesture to our easels and paints and pick up a brush.

For the second time this afternoon, Iris says "Let's doooooooooo it."

The three of us start to paint. There's nothing better than brushing paint onto canvas while ocean waves ebb and flow in front of us and the salty warm breeze wafts around us. Without a doubt, this is my happy place.

"So Rissy, what else have you learned about starfish at school?" I ask while sketching an outline of my five-legged creation.

Iris forgoes sketching and dives right in with huge globs of paint. "They don't have blood, they move using thousands of cute little tube feet, they eat with their stomachs inside-out, and they can make starfish babies two different ways: the sperm and egg way or the regeneration way."

"All true," I say. "Most people love talking about sharks and whales and dolphins, but if you ask me, these little guys are the most fascinating creatures in the ocean."

We fall into a comfortable, peaceful silence as we focus on our paintings.

The baby takes that opportunity to squirm around in my belly. It feels like he's communicating that he's feeling happy and content right now too.

I'm not sure why, but more and more I'm convinced the baby is a boy. Initially, I wanted to find out the sex as soon as possible. It felt like the fewer surprises along the way, the better. But I could tell James loved the idea of finding out on the baby's birthday, so we decided to wait.

I just keep picturing this little boy with my eyes and James's olive skin. A chubby little baby boy with his Daddy's smile and my chin.

My eyes start to water with happy tears. I place my hand on my belly and soak up all the excitement and gratitude I feel at this moment. The doubts and the fear can take a back seat for right now.

Iris's animated voice jolts me from my reverie.

"Whoa, Mom, I just realized something!"

"What's that, Rissy?" Eva says as she streaks a line of orange across her canvas.

"Well, you said with human babies, the sperm and the egg come together, and that's how fertilization happens, right?"

"Right..." Eva says.

"And that the fertilized egg turns into a blastocyst, travels down the fallopian tube to the uterus where it implants and becomes a zygote and then it turns into and embryo and finally a fetus?"

"Right..." Eva says again, then turns to me and quickly whispers, "James told you about all the birds and the bees questions we've been getting from this one lately? We thought it was best to give her the scientific facts and skip all the old-school stork stuff."

"Makes sense to me," I whisper back. "Do parents still use the stork explanation?"

"You'd be surprised!"

"You guys know I can hear you, right?" Iris points a paint-covered brush at us. "You stink at whispering."

"You're right, Rissy," Eva says at full voice and continues to fill in her starfish arms with color. "We stink at whispering. What was your realization, cutie?"

"When I got in your belly it was because Daddy's sperm was inside you, right?"

My eyes go wide.

Eva noticeably cringes.

Maybe we're not as evolved and progressive as we thought.

Eva mouths the word, "Sorry," at me before saying, "Right, baby that's true, but —"

Iris sidles up next to her mom and kisses her sleeping little sister's hair, totally unaware of the awkwardness this discussion is creating. "And then when Daphne got in your belly, it was because *Ron's* sperm was inside you."

"Also true, but honey —"

Iris is on a roll. "And *then*, Daddy's sperm jumped from inside your body to inside of Louise's body to make my new little brother or sister!"

"Geezuz," I say under my breath. When she lays it all out there like that, our little modern family sounds so scandalous.

"Is that all accurate?" Iris's eyes dart between me and Eva, gauging what must be looks of horror on our faces.

I take a much-needed sip of water and gesture to Eva, "Take it away, Mom!"

"Um – yes. That's all accurate, Iris, except for the part where Daddy's sperm jumped from my body to Louise's body. Sperm don't jump from body to body."

"Oh." Her cute forehead wrinkles. "So how did all those millions of sperm get inside Louise?"

I choke on my water.

Eva kindly pats me on the back.

"Did you know that, Louise?" Iris says with seriousness. "Did you know that there can be millions of sperm inside you at the same time?"

Eva takes a deep breath and lets it out. "Hey Rissy Roo? I'm happy to talk you through all the particulars of this topic when we get home, okay? But this is our special 'Painting with the Girls' time, right? So... let's paint!"

"Okay." Iris shrugs and runs back to her easel where she dips the pointy end of her paintbrush into the purple and starts speckling her starfish with little dots.

"Nice purple tube feet, girlfriend!" I praise, trying to get our conversation topic back on track.

She gives a curtsey. "Thank you, Mamalou."

"Oh boy." Eva's nose scrunches as she lifts the sleeping baby higher in her carrier. "Daphne's had a blowout." She checks the sides and peeks down her shirt. "Aaaaand this one went straight through. Lou are you cool to hang solo with Iris for a bit? I have to run home and remedy this situation. I brought a change for her, but not for me."

"Of course, that's cool, but do you want to borrow one of my shirts?" I ask.

"No, no. Thanks, but I think this requires a full bath for both of us. Hey, baby?" she calls to Iris. "Daphne and I are going to pop home to get de-pooped. You be good for Louise until I get back, okay?"

"Okay, Momzy Womzee."

I walk Eva to the screen door and chuckle. "That girl loves her nicknames, doesn't she?"

Eva smiles as she steps inside the house. "She certainly does."

I stay on the back patio so I can keep an eye on Iris.

"I've been meaning to ask you... is that whole 'Mamalou' thing okay with you? I never want to step on toes and — well, I don't really know when or why she started saying that, but —"

"I think it's adorable," Eva says. "And she calls you Mamalou because you're another mother figure to her."

"Is that okay?" I ask again.

"Of course it's okay! It's more than okay." She pauses. "Lou, you could never step on my toes. That's just not who you are. From day one, you've been incredible with her. And with *me* too for that matter. I always knew eventually James would find someone. It's what I wanted for him. I'm just really grateful that person is you."

"That is ..." I struggle to find the words. "That means the world to me."

"Me too, girl."

We attempt a hug, and both laugh when our respective baby bellies get in the way.

"By the way, I'm so sorry about that awkwardness back there," Eva says once she pulls away.

"Nothing to apologize for. You did great," I say.

"Really? Oh, thank you. It's so hard to tell sometimes. I mean she *just* turned eight a few months ago. That feels young for the sex talk, doesn't it?"

I lift my hands and chuckle. "Don't ask me. I have no idea."

She sighs. "She was asking all these questions about how babies grow in bellies, so I figured I'd start with the science of it all. But I was holding off on explaining..." She cringes and continues, "How the sperm get in there in the first place."

"Seeing you struggle with this is actually good for me."

"Oh my God, why?"

"I think I've held you up on this pedestal of perfect parenting. It's good for me to see that maybe not everything comes as easily to you as I think."

She cracks up. "Yeah. Knock me off that pedestal immediately, lady, because the only thing that comes easily to me is loving these little goobers. *That* part is easy. But the rest of it?" She shakes her head and smiles. "The rest of it is a day by day, step-by-step backward stumble on a slippery floor while wearing high heels and a blindfold."

I take in a deep breath and let it all out.

"But don't let that scare you." She places a hand on my shoulder. "Because it's awesome. And we're in it together, right?"

"Yeah." I smile. "I guess we are."

"You know how I know you're going to be a great mom?" she asks.

"How?"

She points at Iris happily painting on the beach. "You already are."

My eyes mist up again. I don't know if it's the pregnancy hormones making me so emotional, or if that is just the kindest, most beautiful thing anyone has ever said to me.

Eva saves me from figuring out how to respond by squeezing my hand. "Alright now I really must get these feces off my skin. I'll grab my bag and see myself out the front."

She closes the screen door and disappears through the house.

I'm watching Iris adding ocean waves to her painting when I realize I haven't checked my phone in a while. Since I've entered this last stage of pregnancy, James is all about being in touch every hour on the hour – "just in case." It's excessive but sweet.

When I pick up my cell, I find three missed calls from him and a series of "where are you?" and "please answer your phone" texts.

Before I can call him back or respond to his texts, I hear vigorous knocking reverberating through the house.

"Rissy!" I shout to my little painting protégé. "I'll be right back, buddy!"

She nods and adds special silver glitter paint to the ocean foam.

The knocking gets louder and wilder as I shuffle through the house. "Coming, Eva! Are you okay? Did you forget something?" I open the door as I say, "I told you, you can just..."

But it's not Eva.

It's my mother.

"...come right inside," I finish my sentence on a whisper.

"Don't mind if I do!" My mother barges past me into the house, then turns and rubs my belly. "My goodness, you're huge! Your handsome fella tells me you're in need of some prenatal TLC. Well, look no further, Wheezy. Mommy's here to take care of you now. But first I have to pee. After that, you can show me to the guest suite!"

"Bathroom is the first door down the hall on the left," a guilty-looking James calls out as he rolls up the driveway with my mother's large red suitcase.

My mother disappears into the bathroom, leaving behind a cloud of perfume and emotional chaos in her wake.

"Guest suite?" I can barely get the words out. I'm so confused and upset.

"I can explain," James says.

But I don't know what in the world he could say to get himself out of this one.

Chapter Four

JAMES

Louise's mom stands beside me holding a pitcher of lychee fruit-infused water. "Would you like some more, Jamesy? You look parched."

"He's not parched, Mom." Louise laughs. "You've been hydrating us all day. And please, you gotta stop it with the Jamesy stuff."

It's been two days since Louise's mom arrived unexpectedly, and she's been waiting on us hand and foot ever since. *Literally.* She gives Louise hand and foot massages every chance she gets, saying they are a crucial part of ensuring the blood flows optimally at this point in her pregnancy.

Is that accurate? I have no idea. But surprisingly, Louise doesn't seem to mind. After the initial shock of seeing her on our doorstep, Louise seems to be enjoying her mother's attentions. They haven't had a single blow-up since she arrived. And other than normal mother-daughter squabbles, I daresay Louise is calmer with her mom present.

"Oh, I thought we call him Jamesy," her mom says. "Mabel, don't you call him Jamesy?"

"I do call him Jamesy, Mrs. Anderson, but I also call my fiancé Bing Bang and my best friends entreprewhores, so you probably shouldn't take your nickname cues from me."

Louise's mom waves one hand in dismissal while she tops off everyone's waters with the other hand. "Forget that stuffy Mrs. Anderson stuff, kids. Call me Carol." Her eyes dart back and forth between Louise and Ralph. "Except for you two cuties. You call me Mom, you hear? And *you*." She rubs Louise's belly and lets her voice go all goofy. "You're going to call me Grandma. Or Mom-mom. Or Gigi. I haven't decided yet."

Calliope's mouth drops open. Ralph presses a finger to her chin to guide it closed again.

These two arrived about an hour ago, right as we were sitting down with Wally and Mabel to assemble traditional lei necklaces for the wedding, so we put them right to work, with no real explanation as to why Carol was here.

"Alright," Calliope announces as she ties a ribbon. "I believe I have completed the final lei. You said it's twenty-five total, right?"

"That's right. Thank you, everybody!" Louise rises from the table and gathers all the flower necklaces. "Mom? You want to help me hang these on the patio?"

"I sure do, sweetheart."

Louise sounds giddy when she looks at me and says, "We're going to spritz them with a water bottle, then store them in ziplock baggies in the fridge until Saturday!"

I try to match her excitement with a toothy smile and a double thumbs-up.

The moment the mother-daughter duo exits out the back door, all eyes are on me.

Calliope whisper-shouts, "James. What the fuck? Story time, please. Now." She turns to Ralph. "Also, I'm assuming *you* didn't know about this?"

"I did not," Ralph says and chugs his lychee-infused water.

"How did this happen? Did you invite her? Is she staying here? Last I heard, Lou told Carol she was a deadbeat mom in the middle of the Bucks County Tavern and vowed to never speak to her again."

"That's not exactly true," I say as I clear the table. "They've been in touch... a little bit. And no, we didn't invite her. She showed up out of the blue. Technically, she's not staying here. She checked into a hotel with Mr. Anderson and your parents when she realized we didn't have space here, but last night, she fell asleep on our couch, and this morning, she woke up at six o'clock and cooked us a gourmet breakfast. I'm as surprised as you are, but it's been pretty positive overall."

"Wait a damn second," Calliope says. "*My* parents are here too?"

I nod and set out three fluffy white towels. "I met Ken and Sue at the airport. They seem lovely."

Calliope shakes her head in displeasure. "They travel together now? Ugh. The parental orgy continues."

"The what?" I set out three empty porcelain bowls, pull a face steamer out from under the couch then plug it in on the breakfast counter, fill it with water, and set it to steam.

"Nothing," Ralph interjects. "Creepy private joke between Callie and me. Are you sure Lou is okay with this arrangement? She does seem oddly happy about it."

"It's weird, right? Honestly, she's been with your mom almost every second since she's arrived, running last-minute wedding errands, going out to lunch... We even took her to our OB-GYN appointment this morning. So I haven't really gotten to dig into the situation with her privately."

I set out three sets of tiny metal tools along with these little roller devices made from green stone. I think they're jade. "Alright," I say as I arrange an assortment of lotions and sprays on a tray. "I think that should do it. Oh! I forgot something."

I jog to the hall closet and pull out three fluffy white robes. I hand one to Wally, one to Ralph, and sling the third one over my shoulder.

"Dude, this is luxe material," Wally says as he runs his hand along the robe.

"Glad you like it, man."

Calliope scans everything I've placed on the table and cocks a brow when Wally starts rubbing the robe fabric against his cheek. "Can I ask an obvious question?"

"Sure." I pick up the jade roller thing and spin it around and around.

"What the hell are you doing?"

"Wally's BroSpa Batchelor party starts in T-minus thirty minutes at Casa James," I say matter-of-factly. "Shouldn't you ladies be on your way?"

"They're doing facials and MANicures!" Mabel claps her hands. "Aren't they adorable? My guy loves a good pampering."

"I really do." Wally opens one of the lotions and gives it a sniff.

A few years ago, Wally had a health scare. Who am I kidding?

It was way more than a scare. It was a two-year bout with cancer that led to him losing forty pounds and his original career on Wall Street. Oh, and a wife. Turns out that career and that wife were never meant for him, and thankfully, he regained his health and those forty pounds. But when you go through something like that and come out on the other side, you never take your body for granted again. At least that's what he's told me. So now, this big burly best friend of mine doesn't give a shit what anyone thinks is "tough" or "manly" when it comes to taking care of himself. Facials, pedicures, salt scrubs... he does it all. So tonight, so do I.

"Wow." Calliope nods in approval. "This *is* an adorable idea." She turns to Ralph. "I was bracing myself imagining you surrounded by strippers tonight."

Ralph wraps an arm around her. "No way, lady. You know you're the only woman I want lap dances from."

"Aw. That's good Ralph-alpha, because your lap is the only one I want to dance on."

Calliope is just swinging a leg over Ralph's hip when Louise and Carol reenter. "Callie?" Louise says. "I am past the nausea pregnancy stage, but if I have to watch you mount my brother right now, I fear the vomiting will return."

"Alright, alright. The mounting can wait." Calliope kisses Ralph and stands. "Well, ladies? Shall we head out? I too have pampering plans for *you*."

Mabel claps her hands again. "How lucky are we, Walla-Walla?" She stands behind Wally, who is still seated and testing all the lotions, and wraps her arms around his neck. "To have such great friends throwing us batchelor and buglorette parties?"

Louise looks at Calliope. "Are we having a *bug*lorette party? What does that even – "

"Mabel had some requests. You'll see."

Carol's phone pings with a text. "Your dad is here to pick me up in the rental," she says to Louise. "Everybody have fun tonight! We have plans with our posse, so I'll get out of your hair." She hugs her purse to her heart as she looks at all of us and takes a deep breath. "But I just wanted to say how nice it's been hanging out with you kids this afternoon. And with you, James and Louise.

These past two days have been really special for me." Her voice chokes up. "I can't tell you what it means to me seeing my children so happy and in love with terrific partners."

"That's... that's really nice, Mom," Louise says. "Ralph? Should we, um. Should we say hi to Dad?"

Ralph looks stunned, but says, "Yeah. Sure. Let's, uh... let's go say hi to Dad."

"I'll come too." Calliope takes Ralph's hand, and they follow his mom out the door.

Louise holds back and waits in the hallway for me.

"Me three!" Mabel shouts. "Long lost reunited families are now my jam!" She leans over to kiss Wally goodbye. "Love you, Bing Bang. I think we're going to go from awkward Dad interaction straight to my buglorette."

"Have fun, Mabey Baby. Two more sleeps till you're officially *mine*," Wally says.

He sounds like he choked on a hairball.

"Oooooooh," Mabel shudders. "He did that growly possessive 'mine' thing from Calliope's books, Jamesy. Did you hear how sexy your friend was just now?"

"I did, yeah." I chuckle as I make my way over to Louise.

Mabel whooshes past us and out the door. "Take notes, sir. Take notes!"

Louise wraps her arms around me and rests her head on my shoulder. "You don't need any notes on being sexy."

"I don't?" I murmur into her hair.

Out of the corner of my eye, I see Wally head into the next room, giving us a moment to ourselves.

What a guy.

"Alone at last," I say.

Just then, the baby kicks so hard I feel it too.

"Or are we?" Louise laughs.

I place my hands on her belly in hopes of feeling more.

"God, women are amazing," I marvel.

"*You're* amazing," she says. "I never thought I'd say this, but thank you for forcing me to spend time with my mother these past two days."

"For the record, the woman forced *herself* into my car. I didn't have much of a choice. And believe me, I would much rather have been spending quality one-on-one time with you the past two days."

"I know," she says. "Me too. But surprisingly, this was exactly what I needed. I didn't realize how much my relationship – or lack of a relationship – with her was weighing me down. Last night, she and I had a really long, really honest talk. I didn't yell this time. She didn't cry. We just listened to each other... for maybe the first time ever." She sighs happily. "Between that and a sweet pep talk from Eva the other day, I'm feeling so much better about things."

"That's great, baby."

A part of me is disappointed I couldn't be the one to help her feel better. But I guess Wally's right. Sometimes we need to work shit out on our own. And far be it from me to question the power of women helping women.

We look out the window where Ralph is shaking their dad's hand and Carol is beaming by his side.

"She wasn't a great mom while I was growing up," Louise says softly. "She knows that. I know that. But that doesn't mean we can't find something positive moving forward." She looks down. "In the meantime, I'm going to put my focus on this little dude."

"*This* little dude?" I point at my dick.

"No, you dork!" She laughs and points at her belly. "I'm going to focus on *this* dude and be the best mom I can be!"

"Of course, of course. Excellent plan." I run my hands down her hair and kiss her forehead. "It was getting pretty serious in here for a minute. Felt like the right time for a dick joke. Was it not the right time for a dick joke?"

"It's always the right time for a dick joke." She kisses me softly on the lips, then looks outside again. "Well, this is a horrifying transition, but with that, it's time for me to say hello to my father."

She grabs her purse and moves to the door.

"You want me to come outside with you? Connect with your dad?"

"Nah. He'll be here all week. Plenty of time for us to chip away at healing that parental relationship too. I'll find a time for us all to sit down together."

As soon as Louise opens the door, Mabel shouts from the driveway, "Hey, Lou! Your parents are coming to the wedding!

Calliope's parents too! Add four more place settings, biotch!"

Louise gives her a thumbs-up.

"Looks like that time will be at the wedding," I say.

"Looks like it." Her eyes widen. "Okay. Have fun with Ralph and Wally. I won't be too late."

She gives me one more kiss and steps outside.

"Hey, Cold Brew?" I call to her before she gets too far.

She turns and smiles at the old nickname. "Yes?"

"You really think we're having a boy, huh?"

"I do." She nods. "Not sure why. Mother's instinct maybe? Oh, and hey." She rushes back to me and whispers in my ear. "For the record? Your little dude..." Her eyes do a quick scan of my body. "...is most definitely *not* little." She pauses. "Tell him I've missed him, will you?"

"He's missed you too," I say, my voice going all growly.

"Well, if he's not busy tonight when I get home, tell him I'd love to have a word with him."

"A word?" I tilt my head to the side. "Or a *conversation*? Because I'm not sure if you remember, but my dude and I can be quite *verbose* when called upon. And it's been way too long since we've *chatted* with you, so we've really built up a lot to *say*, and –"

"Ugh." Ralph suddenly stands beside us looking like he's going to... well.... ralph. "I'm trying not to be that weird, possessive brother, guys, but your sexual euphemisms are grossing me out."

"Don't worry. We're done," Louise says.

"For now," I emphasize and pat him on the back. "Sorry not sorry, Ralph."

Louise walks down the stone path and waves to us. "Love you both. Enjoy your BroSpa!"

I blow her a kiss and guide Ralph into the house. After the door clicks, I ask, "Everything okay out there?"

"Yeah," he says, sounding surprised. "Everything is great. I think things in my family are finally moving in the right direction."

Right then, Wally comes out of the bathroom wearing his fluffy white robe and slippers and rolling that green stone on his face. "You know what's moving in the right direction? My lymphatic system. These jade rollers are incredible."

Let the BroSpa bachelor party begin.

Chapter Five

LOUISE

"*I* don't know, guys," I say. "Two years ago, I could barely dip my toes in the ocean. Now you want me to float for sixty minutes pregnant and alone in a huge vat of pitch-black salt water while stripped of all my senses?"

"And your clothes," Mabel adds. "It's recommended that you also strip away all your clothes. And you won't be alone. We reserved a tank big enough for three."

"*Pregnant and Alone*. Wasn't that a weird reality show a few years ago?" Calliope muses.

Mabel shakes her head. "You're thinking of *Naked and Afraid*. That's still on, and it's magic! Whatever genius decided to create a show combining my two favorite things – nature and nudity – forever has my heart." She turns to me and puts her hands on my shoulders. "But trust me, Lou, you don't need to be naked or afraid right now. They recommend floating in the buff to minimize tactile sensory input, but I figured that might not be your jam. So I stole one of your maternity suits when you weren't looking and shoved it in my buglorette bag. Here you go."

Between all I've been juggling with hosting the wedding and getting ready for the baby, we decided Calliope would be in complete charge of planning the bachelorette. Turns out, Mabel wanted to "float with her besties" in one of those sensory deprivation tanks that are all the rage these days.

"We have to wear antennae," Calliope says with a forced smile.

"You don't *have* to," Mabel corrects. "But I'd certainly *like* you to." She pulls out three headbands with bug antennae from her bag and hands us each one. Calliope and I are good sports and put them on.

"Bing!" Mabel flicks my antenna, and the green ball at the end of the metal spring bounces back and forth. "My dreams are coming true, bitches! I always see people with penis straws and 'Big Boobie Beach Balls' in bachelorette pictures, but I use those things in my everyday life, ya know? So I wanted us to have special props nearer and dearer to my bug-loving heart for my bachelorette. Ooooooh." Mabel shudders happily. "We're going to be like adorable little water striders floating in our tank with our sexy antennae."

"Shall we put on our suits?" Calliope gestures to the changing stalls. "I'm with Lou on this one. I love you both but feel no inherent need to be naked with you."

"Fair enough," Mabel says good-naturedly.

We head into our respective stalls to get changed.

I slip off the sundress I'm wearing and say, "I thought the plan was massages."

"Yeah, we thought about massages," Calliope says from her stall. But it seemed like you didn't love the idea of one more person touching you."

"What gave you that idea?" I ask.

Mabel chimes in, "When we brought up massages, you said, 'Ughhhhhh. I don't want one more person touching me.'"

"You'd just gotten back from that doctor appointment where they were trying to turn the baby," Calliope explains.

"Oh, well that makes sense. That was some invasive shit," I say.

Thankfully, it worked, and the baby is now pointing in the right direction.

Mabel continues, "And then when I asked if the scientist in you was aroused by all the cool sciencey stuff happening inside your uterus, you said, 'Aroused? You think I'm *aroused*? I hate to break it to you, Mabes, but sex is the last thing on my mind right now. I don't want *one more person touching me*.'"

I laugh. "I really don't enjoy the impressions you two do of me. But fine, I get it. I've been a moody pregnant lady. I'm sorry. I've been in a bit of a fog these past few months, but I think I'm coming out of it now."

"Nothing to be sorry for, sister friend. I think you're doing great."

"Me too!" Mabel says. "You're already a much better mother than the walking stick bug. She just dumps her eggs willy-nilly. Doesn't even make sure they're safe from predators or close to a pile of dung for a food source!"

I snort a laugh as I pull my bathing suit over my massive belly. "Well, that's a pretty low bar you're setting for motherhood, Mabes."

"True," Mabel says as she exits her stall in a green and white polka dot bikini. "But you're going to soar above that bar and be even better than the German cockroach. She's known as the best insect mother. She carries thirty to forty eggs around in a little egg purse created from hardened foamy secretions until she finds a safe place for them to hatch. She's awesome, and so are you."

I step out of my stall and rub my belly. "Thank you. I don't have a hardened foamy secretion purse for this little guy, but he seems pretty snug and happy in here."

Mabel claps when she sees me. "Aw, you look so cute! Like you smuggled a big beach ball in your suit!"

Calliope steps out of her stall and says, "Yeah, girl, you look hot! Is it weird to tell a pregnant friend she looks hot?"

"Nope," I say. "It's much appreciated." I take a step toward the tank and peer in the window. "So how does this work? We just… lie down in the water?"

"Yup! It's only twelve inches deep, but it's filled with a gazillion grains of salt, so – in the words of Pennywise in Stephen King's *It* – 'We all float down here.'"

"I'm nervous enough already, Mabes." I chuckle. "No need for scary clown impersonations right now."

Mabel places a hand on my shoulder. "Like I said before, no need to be afraid. Rest assured, Calliope and I went down a whole bunny tunnel of research on this. Floating is awesome for pregnant people."

"You mean a rabbit hole?" I ask.

She purses her lips and looks toward the ceiling. "Hm. Yeah, I guess that's right. But I'm gonna stick with saying bunny tunnel. It's way more fun, don't you think?"

"I do, yeah."

I squeeze her hand. She holds onto mine, opens the door, and guides me into the space holding the tank.

Calliope shuts the door behind us and points at a sign. "Sorry, my buggy bride-to-be. It says 'No jewelry or other accessories while floating in the tank.'"

"Ah, dammit." Mabel puts her hand out to us. "Bugbands need to come off. That's okay. We'll just wear them at the rehearsal dinner tomorrow."

We hand Mabel our antennae, and she places them in a pile on a bench.

"Wow." I take in the spacious tank and the intense level of silence in here. "So we just... get in?"

"They recommend sitting first to get used to the water," Mabel says. "But yeah. After that, you just kick back and relax."

Silently, all three of us step into the warm water and sit down. From this seated position, the water just barely covers my entire belly.

I'm not gonna lie. It already feels like heaven.

"So," Mabel whispers like we're now in a sacred space. "Here are just a few of the health benefits for a pregnant floater – and everyone else for that matter." She counts off on her fingers in the dim light. "Extreme relaxation, stress relief, decreased anxiety, improved sleep, a fast track to a deeply meditative state –"

"Okay, okay, I get it," I whisper back. "Floating will solve all the world's problems." I pause and give them a look. "This is still Mabel's bachelorette party, right? Why do I feel like you guys are doing all this for me?"

They shrug. Almost like they choreographed it.

"We love you, ya punk," Calliope says softly. "And you're about to make us hot aunties. We wanted to make sure to celebrate and support you this week too."

I place my hands on my belly and close my eyes so I don't cry. I'm so lucky.

"One more thing before I turn off the light," Mabel says. "You didn't shave today, did you? They say shaving can cause tiny cuts and abrasions that don't feel so good when the salt water hits 'em."

I laugh. "Lady, I gave up shaving weeks ago when I could no

longer see my feet."

"Okay, good. Lights out!" she whisper-shouts.

Mabel presses a button beside the tank.

We're plunged into darkness.

All three of us lie back and...

We float.

Suddenly, I'm weightless.

Worry-less.

Five minutes into the experience, all I can think is "Oh my God this is some kind of voodoo magic, and I'm in love with everyone and everything."

"I agreeeeeeeeee," Calliope says.

"Shit. Sorry," I whisper. "I didn't realize I was saying that out loud."

"Silence *is* recommended," Mabel whispers beside me. "But since you've broken that rule, I did want to momentarily circle back to something. Is that okay?"

"Circle away, friend."

"Before, when I asked you if you were aroused by the pregnancy experience, that came out weird. I meant to ask if you were *roused*. Not aroused. Like awakened, you know? Gosh, it's just so hard for me to turn off the sexy."

Calliope snorts but otherwise stays quiet.

"You're asking if the pregnancy experience has *awakened* me?" I say.

"Yeah. Wally and I are eventually going down that path, so it's on my mind, I guess. I've heard people say stuff like 'I didn't know who I was until I became a mother,' and 'I feel like my life didn't really begin until my child's did.' I guess I'm wondering if that sort of thing is true."

"Uhhhhhhhhh," I say, holding space while I try to respond in a way that's honest but not judgey. "Those particular sentiments don't really resonate with me. I know who I am. And my life has been full and good for a long time." I hesitate. "But... yeah, in a way, I think this baby has *roused* me. Knowing he or she is on the way has helped me cut some of the self-sabotaging stuff I used to do. Realizing I'm going to be guiding someone else makes me want to let go of the heavier stuff that has dragged me down so I can be lighter for them. And the whole experience has made me really appreciate James. He's a great dad and an incredible partner." I sigh. "Shoving him into that walk-in refrigerator two years ago was the best decision I ever made."

"He'll be awesome in the delivery room too. He definitely won't be one of those guys who faints at the first sight of blood, then needs the whole birth team to focus on resuscitating him while an eight-and-a-half pound bowling ball barrels down Lady Alley."

"Lady Alley?" I say.

"Mabes," Calliope gently scolds. "Don't say stuff that will scare her."

"I'm saying that James *won't* be that kind of guy," Mabel protests. "If I know Jamesy – and I'm pretty sure I do – he'll be the guy who stimulates your nipples if your contractions stall. He'll want to clamp and cut the umbilical cord after it stops pulsing. He'll squirt witch hazel on maxi pads for you and store them in the freezer, so you have something cool and refreshing to shove in your mesh post-partum panties to soothe your potentially torn perineum. I bet if you ask him nicely, he'll even feast on your placenta with you after the birth while you replenish your iron and protein."

"Mabes?" Calliope says more forcefully this time. "I know your intentions are good. They always are. But maybe this conversation isn't the best way for us – especially Louise – to relax."

"You're right, you're right. My apologies, Louise. I'm just so excited for you." Mabel lowers her voice again. "Let's go back to the magical silence now."

"Sounds good," I whisper.

"Can I say just one more thing?" Mabel's voice pops up a few minutes later just as I'm drifting into some sort of watery meditative state.

"Sure," I say.

"No matter how your birth goes, Lou, I know in my heart it's going to be beautiful. Because you are beautiful. In every way. And James adores you. In every way. You'll be an amazing team.

"That's really sweet, Mabes. Thank you."

Plus, you're a mammal," she continues. "And mammals get the birth thing right."

"How do you mean?" I ask.

"I'll likely regret this," Calliope says. "But yeah, what the hell do you mean?"

"Well, no offense to my beloved bugs, but their lives can be so cutthroat – every bug for himself, ya know? And that starts right from the beginning. In the bug world, there's an awful lot of hatching, which is different from birth. It's a lot of quivering and shaking, then quaking and cracking. And that's beautiful in its own way, seeing thousands of little buggies poking their heads out and making their way into the big, wide world. But it's kind of sad too when you think about it. Because there are thousands of them. And they're still alone. Sure, ants and bees and termites are known to work together for the common good when it comes to making honey, creating tunnels, and chewing down people's wooden chair legs, but for the most part, no one's there for them when they're born. And certainly no one cares when they die. But look at mammals! Mammals are a whole different, beautiful ball game. When you're a mammal, your mom is your teammate from day one. That little baby works with its mama so they can be together in this new, exciting way where they look into each other's eyes and make a promise to do life together. It can be an unpredictable and painful ride sometimes, but so worth it. Because on the other side, all that uncertainty is love."

There's a deep silence after that.

I'm filled up with a contented feeling I can't quite describe.

You gotta hand it to Mabel McGonigle. The girl's got layers.

Calliope whispers, "Wow, Mabes. That was..."

"Really beautiful." I finish the sentence for her. "Thank you for that, friend. I'm lucky to have you. To have both of you."

"Mammals unite!" Mabel whispers like the wonderful weirdo she is, and reaches out to us.

All three of us link hands and float.

Before my mind drifts off into peaceful weightlessness, I think about someone else in my life I'm really lucky to have.

And I can't wait to get home to him.

Chapter Six

JAMES

"Who knew pregnancy sex was so hot?" I say in the throes of long overdue passion.

"Is that what we're calling this?" She laughs and runs her hands over my buzz cut in that way that I love. "Pregnancy sex?"

"Well, last time I was lucky enough to be in this situation with you, your belly wasn't so... so..."

"Huge?" she suggests.

"I was going to say so... beautiful. So bountiful. So blissful."

She stops what she's doing and gives me a look. "You're talking weird. Why are you talking weird?"

"Sorry." I brush her hair off her forehead and proceed to nibble down her neck. "After the BroSpa disbanded, I was flipping through that natural birth book on your nightstand. The one called 'Beautiful, Bountiful, Blissful?' I guess it stuck in my head."

"Yeah..." She tips her chin up so I have better access to her neck. "I'm not so sure about that book. The more I ponder our birth plan, the more I'm thinking epidural, epidural, and more epidural."

"Whatever is best for you," I breathe. "You know that. Healthy mom, healthy baby. That's all that matters."

Things start picking up steam again until she says, "Looks like my mom and dad plan on staying on the island until after the baby is born."

"Cool, cool. But maybe don't mention your dad while I'm inside you?"

"Sorry. You're right. Before I forget, though, I love knowing they care and that they're excited, but that doesn't change my mind about who's in the room for the birth. Just you and me."

"Just you and me, baby," I repeat.

"God, I missed this," I say as I continue to pump inside her from behind, my hands caressing her breasts and teasing her nipples.

"I missed it too," she breathes. She reaches a hand behind her and digs her nails into my ass. "I'm close, James. I'm so close."

"I'm right there with you, baby. Come with me. Come with me!"

"Son?" a male voice says. "Son?"

"Whoa, whoa, whoa, whoa, whoa," I say and snap out of my memory from two nights before.

I'm standing on the beach under a wooden arbor covered in Hawaiian orchids while the notes of a live string quartet carry on the ocean breeze.

Louise's father stands in front of me, looking confused.

"Sorry to startle you, kid." He smacks me lightly on the shoulder. "Did I overstep? Is it... too much too soon to call you son?"

"Oh no, no. That's fine, Mr. Anderson. Hi. How're ya doing? Happy you're here."

I reach out to shake his hand. He takes my hand with both of his and looks me deep in the eyes.

"Call me Stan, will ya?"

"Sure," I say. "Stan, it is."

"Thank you, James. Believe me, I'm happy to *be* here. Getting a second chance to be a real part of my family after all the times I —" He can't seem to finish the sentence. He looks beyond the gold-painted chairs where Ralph and his mom are chatting. "Well, it's a gift I never imagined I'd get. And now to be a grandfather too?" He blows out a breath and shakes his head.

"I know it's given Louise a lot of hope having the four of you together in one place again," I say. "Moving forward, right? I'm looking forward to getting to know you better, sir."

"Same here, son." He pauses. "You were somewhere else just now when I walked up. Everything okay?"

"Oh yeah." I chuckle nervously. "Just some Best Man / Minister jitters, I guess. No biggie."

Just then, Louise rushes up to us, her cheeks so flushed they nearly match the pink of her bridesmaid dress.

"Damn, you look adorable!" I say. "But aren't I not supposed to see you before the wedding?"

"The *groom* is not supposed to see the *bride*. The Best Man/Minister can totally see the bridesmaid." She notices her dad standing there for the first time. "Nice suit, Dad. Looking sharp."

"Thanks, kid. I'll go sit with your mother and let you two talk." He nudges Louise gently as he passes, and says, "You got yourself a good one."

"I sure did." She smiles.

"So what's going on?" I ask. "You seem amped."

"Meilani had her baby!" She beams and holds up a live cam on her phone. "Look! She literally had the baby five minutes ago, and she's already nursing her. Isn't that incredible?"

"Wow." On the screen, Meilani lies beside her pup, who drinks milk like a champ.

"Instincts, am I right?" Louise is so excited she's out of breath. "It was wild. I just had this gut feeling to check in on her cam while we were putting the finishing touches on our makeup, and there she was... birthing her baby. She made it look so easy." She sighs happily. "Incredible."

"Sounds like you have some pretty strong instincts too, lady."

Just then, the string quartet launches into "Isn't She Lovely" by Stevie Wonder, and all the guests take their seats.

"That's our cue." Louise gives me a quick kiss. "You're going to officiate the shit out of this wedding. Love you."

"Love you too."

As she makes her way to the end of the aisle, ready to process with Calliope, the groom sidles up beside me.

"Thanks for doing this with me," Wally says.

"Are you kidding me? One of the great honors of my life, sir." I lean forward and peer at his pants.

"What are you doing?" he asks.

"Just checking. Last time you wore white pants outdoors, you showed the whole world you're packin'." I pat him on the back. "We're good, though. Full coverage today."

"Good to know, buddy. Good to know."

Louise and Calliope make their way down the aisle and stand

on the opposite side of the arbor. I give my lady a wink.

The quartet crescendos into the chorus, and Mabel appears, looking as beautiful and happy as I've ever seen her, flanked by both her dads: the one she grew up with and her birth dad, who she's just getting to know.

I look out over the attendees. There's not a dry eye in the house. Or rather, on this beach. The worst offender is the groom, who already has big wet tears rolling down his cheeks.

It's awesome to see.

When Mabel reaches Wally, and they join hands, I launch into the service.

"Dearly beloved, we are gathered here today to –"

Wally and Mabel whip their heads around and stare at me like I've lost my mind.

"Kidding!" I say. "I'm kidding everyone. When two beautiful weirdos like Wallace and Mabel get hitched, two things are guaranteed. One? Anything can happen. And two… nothing that happens will be stuffy or traditional."

Louise's eyes go wide at that. And I swear she's trying to get my attention.

I continue, "With that said, our couple would like to start the ceremony with a little step back in time to remind us all how their love story began. Take it away, Mabel."

I move out of the way and plant myself next to my girlfriend.

"Walla-Walla Bing Bang. When we first met, I thought you were a sexy psycho-killer who buried people in his backyard…"

I lean close to Louise and whisper as quietly as I can, "You okay? You look like you've seen a ghost."

She whispers, "Looks like Meilani isn't the only one having a baby today."

"What do you mean?" I ask.

"My water just broke."

Chapter Seven

LOUISE

*M*y legs have a mind of their own.

Voices call behind me as I hustle down the beach, and I know I should acknowledge them, but the only thing going through my mind is "get to the water."

All the articles said first-time babies rarely come early, and their labors are usually long.

According to those articles, there would be all sorts of signs telling me I was getting close to go-time. My ligaments would feel loose. I'd pass something horrifying called a mucus plug. I'd feel a sudden need to *nest* and clean and organize. And once the contractions started, they would build slowly and predictably, so much so that my birth partner would even be able to clock them.

Well, those articles were wrong.

Because in a rush to make his appearance three weeks early, this first-time baby didn't give me any sort of heads-up about his plans.

I've never liked the way birth is depicted in movies. It's always this chaotic event where women are rushed to hospitals, screaming and yelling in fear and agony. If it's a drama, there's inevitably a terrifying moment when the mom or the baby might not make it. If it's a comedy, we get bumbling, fainting fathers and birthing women who grab men by the collar and growl, "This is all your fault, asshole."

My experience right now is something else entirely.

It's presence.

It's calm.

It's a deep knowing that I can do this. That my baby and I were made for each other, and we can do anything together.

Get to the water.

James catches up to me just as I reach the edge of the ocean and stare out over the water. "Hey," he says, out of breath. "Talk to me. What's going on? What do you need?"

"You're supposed to be marrying Wally and Mabel," I say through an intense contraction.

"Don't worry about that. You're what matters right now." He places a hand on my lower back. "What are we doing? Are we calling the doctor?"

"No time." I squeeze the words out right just as the most intense pressure I've ever felt in my life rocks my lower body. I bend my knees and squeeze the hell out of James's forearms.

"No time? What do you mean no time?" he says.

I freeze.

James squats down and looks up at me, his forehead creased and his breathing heavy. "What, baby, what?"

The ocean waves continue their frothy ebb and flow.

A single seagull caws overhead.

But I'm silent.

"Seriously, Lou. Talk to me, please."

"James?" I finally whisper.

"Yeah?"

"Can you do me a favor?"

"Of course! What? Anything!"

"Can you... look between my legs? Because I'm pretty sure the baby's head is there."

"Are you fucking kidding me right now?" he yells.

"Shh. Shh. Shh. It's okay. Everything's okay. But no, I'm not kidding." I take a deep breath and let it out. "Completely serious right now."

James drops to his knees in silence. It's at that moment I notice that his tan suit is the same color as the sand. He gingerly lifts the skirt of my satin pink bridesmaid dress... then immediately places it back down.

He swallows. "I, um. I just saw our kid. Our kid is there."

"Yeah, that's what I thought," I say.

Another contraction overtakes me. James supports me as I lower myself to the ground. To call these sensations painful would be a drastic understatement. But, somehow, the pain isn't what I focus on.

It's the power moving through me that has my attention.

"Is it pushing time? Oh my God, are we pushing?" James positions himself between my legs, his breaths continuing to come out in short bursts like he's the one in labor, not me.

"We are," I say calmly. "We're pushing."

When I say "we," I mean it in the greatest sense of the word. I've never felt more supported, more connected. To James, absolutely. But to my baby as well. And to these intense waves of energy pulsing through me.

As I ride the next contraction and push along with it, I keep my eyes on the ocean waves in front of me, rising and falling, pushing and pulling just like I am.

At this moment, we're the same.

I am the ocean, and the ocean is me.

I'd have a hundred more babies if it means feeling this powerful and intentional.

This present.

Okay, scratch that. Those are absolutely the hormones talking. One, maybe two kids will do, but... wow.

This moment is everything.

I push and push and push.

And then a baby cry mixes with the sound of the surf.

It's the most beautiful thing I've ever heard.

"I got her, Lou. I got her!" James says, a mess of happy tears.

"*Her*?" I say.

"Yeah, her," he beams. "It's a girl."

James hands our tiny, squirming daughter to me.

I hold her tight to my chest and whisper, "Nice to meet you, baby girl. I'm your mom."

She immediately settles when she hears my voice, and I swear to God, she holds me back.

James looks farther up the beach where Mabel and Wally and the whole party of wedding guests are waiting for the good news. "It's a girl!" he shouts to them.

Everyone whoops and cheers.

James wraps his arm around me and kisses me on the forehead. "You're incredible, Lou. I'm in absolute awe of you right now."

"Me too!" I laugh and cry at the same time.

"You know we need to head to the hospital and get you both checked out," he says softly.

"Yeah, I know." I look out over the ocean where the sun is starting to set. "But can we stay here just a moment longer?"

"Absolutely." He peers over his shoulder, then turns back to me. "Can I bring Iris down here with us? Is that okay?"

"Of course!" I smile. "Please. Get her down here."

James gestures to Eva to let Iris come to us.

A moment later, a series of excited footsteps press into the sand, and Iris sits down beside us. Her eyes are filled with wonder.

"It's a girl?" she squeals quietly, already such a kind and sensitive sibling. "I have another little sister?"

"You sure do, kiddo." I turn to James and laugh. "I guess my instincts were off on that one, huh?"

"Fine by me," he says, then moves Iris onto his lap and pulls me even closer.

"Yeah? Think you can handle being surrounded by all us girls?"

"Are you kidding me?" James says with tears in his eyes. "Surrounded by you ladies for the rest of my life?" He leans over and presses the softest kiss on our little miracle's head. "That's my idea of heaven."

$\mathcal{E}$pilogue

LOUISE

"Happy Birthday, Marin!" our friends and family shout happily. We're all standing in a semi-circle on the beach, the oranges and pinks and reds of the sunset all around us as we watch our chubby little girl trying to blow out the birthday candle on her strawberry cream cupcake. When she doesn't quite make it, her big sister, Iris, saves the day and adds some extra breath power into the mix.

Everyone claps and laughs when Marin smashes her whole cute face into the icing and enjoys her first bites of cake.

James runs a hand up and down my back.

"How is she one?" I shake my head in disbelief.

"Time flies, doesn't it?" he says.

"It sure does."

"Walk with me?" James whispers in the voice that means he wants to get me alone.

Alone time has been increasingly difficult to come by since I became a mom.

"Hold on just a sec," I whisper back.

I jog over to my mom and ask if she'll watch Marin for a few minutes while James and I take a walk on the beach. Her whole face lights up, and she agrees immediately. Our relationship has come such a long way over this past year. After the baby was born – in surprising and spectacular fashion – my mom and dad stayed local for a whole month and helped however they could. She and I finally opened that box that had been sitting sealed in our living room for months. My mom gifted me a beautiful new set of paints, which we used together to finish Marin's seascape mural in the nursery.

James and I are a few steps into our walk when I turn to see my mother cleaning my daughter's cheeks and snuggling her in her arms.

"I'm so glad I didn't give up on her." I thread my fingers with his.

"I'm so glad you didn't give up on *me*," James says.

"What? When was I ever going to give up on *you*?" I laugh because it's ridiculous.

"When I dirty-talked you like a dork during our one-night kegstand? When I got you kicked out of Mabel's apartment by almost killing her praying mantis during another bout of sexy time? When I cried watching *Splash*? When I was a nervous mess during Marin's birth, and you stayed cool as a sea cucumber?"

I snort. "The first few things you mentioned, I could deal with. But I may have to leave you for that terrible sea cucumber joke you made just now."

He laughs. "That would be understandable."

I smile and plant a quick kiss on his delicious lips. "You're the best thing that's ever happened to me. Don't you ever forget it. No chance you're getting rid of me now, buddy. You're stuck with me for life."

"Music to my ears, Cold Brew."

He pulls me into his arms and kisses me slow and deep.

"Are you guys always this graphic during family-friendly affairs?" Wally is suddenly beside us, with Mabel, Calliope, and Ralph following close.

"Seriously!" Mabel laughs. "If you're not expelling human beings out of your nether regions at weddings, you're shoving your tongues down each other's throats and groping butts at babies' birthday parties!"

James lifts the offending hand from my butt and holds it up in defense. "First of all, the sometimes-nudist has no room to talk." Calliope and Ralph are cracking up too. He points at them next. "Neither do the mile-high-clubbing museum exhibitionists. And second... we thought we were alone."

Calliope picks up a seashell and tosses it back in the ocean. "Your friends are leaving tomorrow, ya punks! Excuse us for thinking you'd like to spend us much time with us as possible before we fly nearly five-thousand miles away from you again."

"Aw, I don't want you to go," I pout and bring Calliope and Mabel in for a girl hug.

"You guys are in for Friendsgiving in Philly, right?" Ralph asks James and me. "That's less than three months away."

"I'll be there for you..." James tries and fails to sing the *Friends* theme song. My man can't carry a tune if his life depends on it.

"What the hell was that?" Wally laughs.

"Ever since becoming a father for the second time, James's dad jokes have reached the tipping point," I explain. "It's an issue. But he's working on it, aren't ya, bud? What he meant to say was, 'Yes. We wouldn't miss Philly Friendsgiving for the world.'"

James nods. "What she said."

"That's awesome," Ralph says. "Because I need to see my niece as much as possible."

"And your sister too, I hope?" I say.

"Eh." He shrugs, then smiles.

Mabel gasps. "How have I never considered this before? Louise! You and Ralph are our Monica and Ross!"

My brother and I both give Mabel a blank look.

"Like in our friend group!" she explains and gesticulates. "You're the siblings in our friend group!"

"Does that make me Rachel Green?" Calliope asks hopefully.

"And me Chandler Bing?" James says.

Mabel claps and squeals. "Yes and yes! Could this *be* any more fun?"

Ralph clears his throat. "Mabes? Enter the *Friends* discussion at your own risk. Calliope isn't shy about expressing her incendiary thoughts on that excellent show. And once she gets started, it's really hard to get her to stop."

"Calliope isn't *shy* about anything," Calliope retorts, referring to herself in third person. "And I certainly take no offense about you being the Ross to my Rachel, Ralph-alpha."

She boops him on the nose, and he pulls her in for a kiss.

Mabel gasps again. "Guys! Ross was a paleontologist too!" Then she double gasps. "And he and Rachel banged in a planetarium just like you! These similarities are blowing my bug-loving mind!"

"To be fair," Calliope says, "While Ralph did work in the planetarium, technically we banged in the dinosaur room."

"Okay!" I interject. "No one needs to hear that story again." I pause and look at James's best friend. "So I guess Wally is Joey," I conclude.

"How *you* doin'?" Wally plays along.

"And Mabel, you are *definitely* Phoebe," I state the obvious.

"Oooooooooh." Mabel shudders happily. "I don't know why, but that just gave me goose pumps. I love Phoebe!"

"Sorry, did you just say goose pumps?" I ask.

"Yeah," Mabel says. "You know, like… good-feeling tingles."

Wally wraps an arm around his wife. "Mabey Baby, those are actually called goose *bumps*."

"No way!" she shouts.

Calliope huffs. "Mabel. All this time, you thought people were saying goose pumps? *Pumps*? As in a goose *pumping* all over your skin?"

"Like a goose *bumping* you is any better?" Mabel cocks her head to the side. "Actually, I guess it is a little better. Anyway, we're getting off topic."

"I wasn't aware there *was* a topic." Calliope chuckles.

"The topic is how much we love each other and how much we're going to miss each other after this trip is over," Ralph says. His voice is all choked up, and it could be my imagination, but his eyes are glassy too.

Wally scoffs. "What's with all the sentimental touchy-feely stuff, people? We're acting like we're never going to see each other again."

Ralph shakes his head. "I don't know, man. I became an uncle, and now I'm suddenly sentimental as shit. But I've also been told that I am a cinnamon roll by nature, so…" He shrugs.

"Really?" James's brow furrows. "Why a cinnamon roll?"

"It's a sexy thing, don't worry," Calliope answers for him.

"Why would I be worried?" James says.

"Because you're one too." She winks.

"On that note," I say," I'm hungry. Who wants cake?"

This is not a group that turns down cake, so the decision to return to the party is immediate and unanimous.

We start the walk back in relative silence until Wally rumbles, "Dare I ask what baked good *I* am? Because I can think of way hotter pastries than cinnamon rolls."

"Let's hear 'em, fella," Calliope says.

"Éclairs. Donuts, the ones with holes of course –"

"Gross." I laugh.

"A good ol' classic almond horn. And, oh God, what are those crunchy tubular things called?"

"Crunchy tubular things?" Mabel says sweetly, ever the supportive wife.

"They're French, I think?" Wally says. "They have crème on the inside and sometimes chocolate chips 'n' shit on the outside?"

"You're thinking of cannoli," James says. "Cannoli are Italian."

"Yes! Cannoli! Cannoli are sexy. Can I be a cannoli?"

As we walk along the sand arm in arm, laughing and poking fun at each other, I can't help but wonder how I got this lucky. To be raising a family with this amazing man by my side. To have this incredible crew of friends. To wake up every day in a place I love, surrounded by love.

It's more than I ever could have asked for.

I look over my shoulder at the wide, beautiful ocean spread out before me and feel nothing but gratitude.

And I can't wait for the adventures life takes us on next.

Backstage Pass

The *Natural History Series* is officially complete! It's bittersweet saying goodbye to this crew of characters.

At some point when I wasn't looking, they became my pals, which is probably what made these novellas so fun and satisfying to write. I knew these characters so well that I could really let them go wild. It was also very cool to have the opportunity to show some more layers to certain characters.

Namely, Calliope.

When I wrote *Flirtasaurus*, I was feeling burned out by how rough we can be on Romance heroines (and on women in general). The idea that male characters can be as grumpy and jerky as they like and still be worthy of love while the women can't make a single misstep was a major bummer to me. So, like the naïve first-time novel-writer I was, I went balls-to-the-wall in the opposite direction. Calliope would be a full-fledged jerk. Suck it, everybody! I went super broad and in-your-face with that book, and I have zero regrets. Because it was FUN, and it opened me up to a whole new world. That said, these novellas felt like a cool opportunity to discover more nuance in that controversial lady. I certainly wanted to stay true to her sass and what a punk she is at her core, but I was interested in showing the doubts and insecurities she has under all that bravado. Ya gotta figure that someone who fights that hard for respect and success is likely worried that on some level she doesn't actually deserve it, right? So, taking Calliope to a nerve-wracking big book signing and watching her question her place in the book world felt just right. It was also a fun opportunity to let "cinnamon roll" Ralph go off the rails. Did you listen to the audiobook? Hearing Jason Clarke perform a dinosaur sex scene inside an erupting volcano is most definitely – as Ralph would say – a treat for your earholes.

Mabel.

Mabel, Mabel, Mabel.

I love her so damn much. When I wrote *Lovebug* I wanted to

explore a heroine who was relentlessly positive. I remember when I was a young actor in my early twenties, a teacher I was working with commented on how happy I seemed and what a lovely actor I was. This sounded like a compliment until she followed it up with, "but you'll never be truly great until you suffer more." I knew immediately that was a crappy worldview to bring to a young person. Plus, I'd already experienced some solid suffering in my life, but I chose to look on the bright side. As I'm writing this, I'm realizing for the first time that even though I left that mentor, I still spent the next seven years seeking and playing sad, crying girls onstage. Some part of me must have believed that tragedy truly was the path to great art. Well, I certainly snapped out of that thinking, huh? ☺ Years later, my doorway into any project I write is comedy. I like to hit more serious topics, but, for me, those moments are so much better when we're allowed to laugh too. Because isn't that the way life works? We laugh at funerals sometimes. We cry at happy birthday parties and anniversaries. It all blends together. Anyway, back to Mabel. I promise this all relates to her. In *Lovebug*, she was a twenty-three-year-old happy-go-lucky girl, just like I was back in that acting class. I didn't want to saddle Mabel with suffering like it was some necessary badge of honor. But... great stories need conflict, right? So, as the writer, it was my job to mess with her and make her squirm in *Lovebug*. In these "Where Are They Now?" novellas however, we're deep in the couples' HEAs (aka Happily Ever Afters). I gotta give you *some* conflict of course, but I don't think readers want to worry about them too much, so I used this as an opportunity to let life pile more and more weird joy onto Mabel. And oh my God it was fun! Speaking of weird joy... narrating that improvised singing stuff in the Netherlands? Holy crap. As soon as I finished, an overwhelming feeling of "What have I done?" washed over me. This was tricky stuff. Because it had to be bad to be good, ya know? I couldn't create some lovely song and try to perform it well. That would be boring, I think. And not the right kind of weird. Plus, do we really think Mabel has some secret song writing genius living inside her? I don't. So, I challenged myself to truly improvise the song in the moment in her less-than-awesome singing voice. I'd already written the words, but I believed strongly that the melody had to come – or not come – right there in the booth. I felt vulnerable and ridiculous – I immediately ran to my readers group and asked for preemptive forgiveness – but I think that energy ended up being just right.

Louise is the trickiest gal of the bunch. I always have this impulse to push her into broad romantic comedy territory, so she "fits in" with Calliope and Mabel, but she inevitably pushes back and says, "But that's not who I am, bitch!" Just kidding. She doesn't literally call me a bitch. But she does rebel by getting quiet on me, which any writer can tell you is *not* the energy you want when you're on a deadline and trying to put tens of thousands of words down on the page. I had lots of stops and starts while writing *Sharkbait*, because Louise and I were wrestling so much. She's tricky. In the series, she is great at observing and counseling other people, but she doesn't love it when the attention is on her. So, I guess it shouldn't be surprising that when I write her as the main character, she messes me and says, "But I told you I don't like attention, bitch!" Okay, I'm done with the bitch stuff. I love Louise. Now and forever. She's taught me so much. Characters really do have minds of their own and they don't like being forced to be someone they're not. Who does? Once I remember that and show her the respect she deserves, Louise always has surprising things to tell me. And experiencing that back-and-forth with creative flow is why I got into this writing game in the first place! I'm proud of her stories. Like she said about her mom, "I'm glad I didn't give up on her." Or, more to the point, I'm glad *she* didn't give up on *me*.

Lastly but not leastly (yes I know leastly is not a word), I loved that these novellas meant we could hear from James again and I could explore Ralph and Wally's POV for the first time! I'm so grateful Teddy Hamilton, Jason Clarke and Joe Arden sign on to do weird stuff with me in audio. I could not be more in love with what they did on this book. They just "get" me, and that's a gift I never take for granted. Thanks dudes! Side note: When I first saw the audiobook cover with our four names on it as the narrators, I thought, "Hmm. Listeners won't think this is a reverse harem, will they?" But then I thought, "Nah. They know me better than that." ☺

Thank you for taking this journey with me, friends! It's been one
hell of a ride. Catch ya on the next one.

xoxo

Erin

About the Author

ERIN MALLON is a romantic comedy author, an award-winning narrator of over 600 audiobooks and an accomplished playwright and producer in New York City. She has written over 40 plays, which have been produced Off-Broadway and all over the country. Erin lives in a little yellow house on the outskirts of NYC with her husband and Three J's.

CONNECT WITH ERIN

Subscribe to my Newsletter: www.erinmallon.com/home#connect
Join My Readers Group: Erin Mallon's Feisty Fitzies!

Website: www.erinmallon.com
Instagram: @mallonerin
Tiktok: @erinmallonwriter
Twitter: @ErinMallon
Facebook: @ErinMallonWriter
Goodreads: www.goodreads.com/Erin_Mallon
Bookbub: www.bookbub.com/profile/erin-mallon

Other Titles by Erin Mallon

The Natural History Series

Flirtasaurus
Lovebug
Sharkbait

Novellas

Showmancing the Bone

Scripted Stories in Audio

These Walls Can Talk
These Walls Can Talk 2: The Narwhal Strikes Back!
These Walls Can Talk 3: Rise of the Machine
The Bromantic Comedies
The Net Will Appear
Skin Hungry
Come Find Me
Branched
Pale Blue Dot(s)